Migration Songs

Migration Songs

Anna Quon

Invisible Publishing

Halifax & Toronto

Library and Archives Canada Cataloguing in Publication

Quon, Anna L., 1968-
        Migration songs / Anna Quon.

ISBN 978-0-9782185-6-0

        I. Title.

PS8633.U65M54 2009   C813'.6   C2009-905186-9

Designed by Megan Fildes
Cover illustration by Sydney Smith

Typeset in Laurentian and Slate by Megan Fildes
With thanks to type designer Rod McDonald

Printed and bound in Canada

Invisible Publishing
Halifax & Toronto
www.invisiblepublishing.com

We acknowledge the support of the Canada Council for the Arts which last
year invested $20.1 million in writing and publishing throughout Canada.

Invisible Publishing recognizes the support of the Province of Nova Scotia
through the Department of Tourism, Culture & Heritage. We are pleased
to work in partnership with the Culture Division to develop and promote
our cultural resources for all Nova Scotians.

Tourism, Culture and Heritage

Canada Council   Conseil des Arts
for the Arts   du Canada

For my grandmother,

(Quon Tse Sui Sieng)

One

I want to remember the day I was born, that rainy day in September. My parents have told me the story so many times that I can feel my mother's hands on me, slippery with afterbirth. There is a stench of lightning, a hot smell from inside my mother's body. But in her hands, I am cooling, becoming solid. Becoming real, like a photo in fixing solution, shedding all other possibilities.

My mother was out in the yard in her rubber boots and rain poncho, picking late summer tomatoes for supper. She bent over to grasp one and when she straightened up, something dropped, like an elevator inside her plummeting toward the ground floor. It was her water breaking. "And you," my mother likes to say, "the one who pushed the elevator button, were not far behind."

There was no time to get to the hospital. My mother leaned against the kitchen table, holding her belly in one hand and the phone in the other. She called my father, who worked as a hospital administrator, and told him to come home. As usual on a Saturday, he was catching up on his paperwork, but he arrived soon after, ahead of the ambulance, which just goes to show how fast he must have driven our battered old Chrysler.

Breathless, his dark hair plastered to his head from the rain, he found my mother sitting on the kitchen floor in a sticky pool, which clung to the soles of his boots as he came to her.

She cradled me, her first-born child, between her legs, the umbilical cord still intact, and looked at him with what my father describes as a mixture of astonishment and accusation, as if she could not believe what had just happened, and was blaming my father for it.

My mother remembers it slightly differently. "I held your little head in my hands and when I looked up, there was your father standing soaking wet in the doorway with his mouth open. He'd forgotten his briefcase. You looked so alike, him with his red face and hair stuck to his head, and you with yours, that I was astonished—your father is right about that. It was as if I held in my arms your father's younger self, although in the form of a girl."

"Help me cut the cord, then," she told my father, who continued to stand there, gaping. Like a stranger, she told me later in private, who'd just happened on the scene. But then the ambulance arrived, with Dr. Jamieson, our next-door neighbour, close behind, poking his head around the doorframe. My father was pushed helplessly aside to hover in the background while the doctor and the ambulance attendants took care of my mother and me. My mother often says that instead of her going to the hospital to have me, the hospital came to her, "including the ambulance, doctor and even the administrator." It is her one brilliant joke. My father smiles each time, or maybe grimaces is a better word. My mother claims I was in such a hurry to arrive that I left my briefcase behind, which she can sometimes feel floating around inside her, like a lost piece of luggage. She says the briefcase contained my instruction manual, and without it she wasn't sure how to raise me, but, she says, she figures she did all right.

I am not so sure. At twenty-nine, I am a nervous wreck—a train wreck of a human being. For one thing, I'm addicted to cough drops, and I haven't been able to keep a job for more than six months. Because of that, I've moved back home with my parents. My father is retired, and after working for three decades at progressively more senior administrative positions at the hospital, he can't understand why I drift from job to job, and why I am now struggling to keep my current one as an elementary school bus driver. A bus driver, for Christ's sake— that's what I hear him thinking, behind his study door in the evening.

My father is an Englishman, with the black hair and blue eyes of an Irishman, which earned him some teasing as a boy. He's been in Canada since before I was born, but he still refuses to sing "O Canada" or pledge allegiance to the queen—he's anti-monarchy and fancies himself a Socialist. He grew up in York, in a working class family, and was the first of his clan to go to university. There he studied classics and literature, much to his own father's concern. But because my father could spell and because he was a good typist, he was never short of work after he graduated and moved to London. At his first job he made more money than his own father ever had.

My father met my mother in 1970 in Hyde Park. There was a crowd of students gathered around a young Chinese man with a bullhorn, who was shouting, "Long live Chairman Mao." He also shouted some other things, but his accent was so thick it was hard to understand him, my father says. My mother was standing in the crowd a few feet away, with a bemused smile on her face. She was, says my father, as lovely as a lotus blossom, her black hair hanging limp and impenetrably dark, her cheeks flushed from the damp air. Her features were Chinese, he says, but instead of Socialist drab she wore an orange mini dress. When she thrust her arm out to salute Chairman Mao, my dad swears she was in fact mouthing the words "Long live the Queen!" She glanced over at him and he was transfixed.

My father doesn't sit with my mother and me watching the news on TV after dinner any more, but goes directly to his study. Just the fact that he even has a study in this day and age is a clue to what kind of man he is. Private. Retiring. Well-read. On special occasions, he smokes a cigar in there and the smooth scent of it creeps out from under the study door. The aroma of my father's absence.

There was a time when his study was a special place where I could come to sit, in a leather chair with brass studs all around the seat, and read a book from his shelves. They were mostly far over my head, swimming with small print and big words that I didn't know. My father would nod approvingly, as if just by opening one of those books, the magic of knowledge would rub off on me.

On his fortieth birthday, my father invited me in to his study. He put the painted rock paperweight that I had made him as a gift on the corner of his desk, and leaned back in his chair, appraising me. He seemed satisfied. His dark eyes were warm with tenderness, something that I did not often see— for the most part he was a handsome man, to my mind, but there always disappointment lurking in him, which made him appear sad and awkward. He handed me his cigar.

"Don't tell your mother," he whispered and seemed happy, almost buoyant. I held it in my hands then put it to my mouth and inhaled.

My father later told me that I turned green before throwing up on his Persian rug. All I remember is feeling queasy, and then I was lying on the floor, staring up at the ceiling. My father was standing over me, with a perplexed and concerned look. It is the same look he gives me now that I am almost thirty and teetering on the edge of unemployment.

In high school, I started to drift off course, though at first even my mother didn't realize anything was wrong. My friends were abnormally bright and sarcastic, bored with the world and at the same time, diligently keeping their marks up. I didn't realize that what I thought of as their ennui and alienation, which I admired, were a teenage occupation, not meant to last. Conventional and timid, I took up the cause of boredom and apathy with gloomy enthusiasm, and gradually lost myself in them.

My parents expected me to go to university, to make something of myself—an accountant, or even a doctor or a lawyer. I remember my father at my graduation, standing with his arm around my shoulders, admiring my diploma. The school principal, a jovial, big-bellied, middle-aged man, came up to us and asked, in a booming voice that made other parents and students turn and look, "So, Joan, what letters are you going to be putting after your name?" I felt the blood creeping into my cheeks. "MD? PhD?" he bellowed. He slapped me on the back and my father looked at me and beamed.

Sometimes I catch my father looking at me over the top of his paper at breakfast, his dark eyes pained, incredulous. As if to say, what are you doing here? What are you doing?

My mother still works at the supermarket. She's a bookkeeper but sometimes she fills in on cash when one of the girls is sick. She was the one who suggested I take a year off after high school, to "find myself." She was probably uneasy with how much time I was spending in my room, staring out the window when I was supposed to be studying. She probably sensed the unhappiness at my core, which bloomed like a dark, night-loving flower.

Well, I had lost myself all right, but finding myself was not going to be as easy as finding a pair of keys. Retracing my steps only leads me back through a series of dim, low-ceilinged rooms, until I emerge into full sunlight at about age eight. Backward from there each year is like a brilliant capsule, well defined, glowing with promise. But although I have tried, I cannot bring those luminous days forward. Once I step back into the house of my future, I am overcome with the dank musty smell of things left lying in the dark, of decay and erosion.

My therapist, Dr. Bard, is an unreasonably bubble-headed optimist. When I show up for my appointment, he bounces to the door to greet me, ushering me in with a smile that says, "I'm so glad to see you." Tall and lanky, with a dark beard and moustache, there is something wounded and sensitive about his doggedness.

He lets me arrange myself in the easy chair across from him. Then he leans forward in his chair, with his hands folded together on his desk, and his index fingers pointing somewhere in the region of my forehead. Still smiling brightly, he waits for me to say something.

I clear my throat. "Well..." I say.

He leans forward eagerly. "Yes?" he asks. I look up at the ceiling. Like a puppy with a ball that is too big for it, he tries again. "Well, how was your week?" he asks.

"It was...fine."

He pounces. "Well, tell me about it!" The last thing I want to do is to tell him about it. My mother pays for me to come here and sit in his office, which I do, but that is all.

Dr. Bard thinks there is something preventing me from "healing my past," which is interfering with my ability to get on with my life. Actually, he has never said this. I have imagined him thinking it, though, as he tries to guide me through self-hypnosis, back into my childhood, which he wants me to reclaim. All the while I sit there with my eyes closed, feeling self-conscious and miserable, pretending to follow his instructions. Occasionally, though, I forget myself, and end up in those early years, where I am no longer a stranger to my own life.

For so long, it was my parents' story that gripped me, over-shadowing my own. My life has always been merely a tendril off the vine of theirs, creeping toward the sunshine. It never bothered me to be a sideshow, an afterthought. But something calls to me from the future—a bird sound, like that of geese in flight, faint but insistent—a song of remembering, pushing out feathers I never knew were mine.

Two

My mother's parents never spoke to her in Chinese. For although they wished Gillian to be a good Chinese daughter, they also wanted her to feel at home, to be just like everyone else in this huge, empty country. The fact that these two desires were opposed to one another, and that Gillian was destined to fulfill neither, would always be a source of unhappiness for her and her parents. Gillian would pass their unease and disappointment down to her own daughter like a genetic trait—and maybe early on, perhaps from before my memory begins, they blighted my own happiness.

Gillian was born in Vancouver and grew up in Nova Scotia, where her father, Foon Fui, worked in a restaurant owned by a distant relative and her mother, Wei Ying, was a seamstress. The Wongs lived in China until not long before the Communists came to power. They left their house in the village, gave their animals to a favourite sister and locked the gate behind them, never looking back. In Hong Kong, they sold their jewellery and worked in the restaurant of a family friend, until they had money to pay for their passage to Vancouver. On the boat ride over, Wei Ying was violently sea sick, or so she thought. In fact she was pregnant with Gillian, who was conceived somewhere over the Pacific Ocean. Foon Fui and Wei Ying were rocked in their bunk by the dark swell of the ocean, gently bringing their daughter into being.

They almost never spoke of those times. It was as though they had put their former lives in a drawer and lost the key. Only once did Wei Ying tell Gillian the story of their passage to North America—to shut her up once and for all—and then, grimly, turned toward the kitchen sink, her back to her daughter. As if to say, you have been told, never mention it again. Perhaps that is why Gillian spent so much time mulling over the history of her life before and after she married. Trying to make sure the puzzle pieces were all there, reminding herself that despite the void of her past, she really did exist.

Perhaps her parents' silence on their story is the reason Gillian was compulsive about telling her own story. Tales, real and invented, confessions divulged to me over the years, and the silences in between—I held onto it all as though my life depended upon it. It did not worry me that what I had was half truth and half invention. Mirrors become fogged and mottled over time anyway; we mould the things that we keep in our hearts to the shape of our own desires—or our own bitterness.

My parents' story began like a fairy tale—or perhaps, it could be said, a fantasy, to cure boredom. Gillian was quite a bit younger than David. When they met in Hyde Park, she was a mere nineteen, and he was thirty. At her parents' command, she was visiting her Aunt and Uncle Wah in Britain, who were to introduce her to a second cousin, "a good Chinese boy," whose father owned a restaurant and who was studying to be a pharmacist. Gillian was happy to take an all-expenses-paid trip abroad, but she doubted meeting the pharmacy student would make much of an impression on her. From his photo, she thought he looked a bit like a scarecrow, rail thin with a shock of black hair and a solemn air that was out of place in a casual snapshot.

He turned out to be a nice, shy young man with whom Gillian was quickly bored stiff, and one day when she was supposed to meet up with him after a class, she wandered off to Hyde Park in the hopes of hearing something radical and dangerous. While she stood listening to the Chinese students bellowing praise of Chairman Mao through a bullhorn, she felt someone staring at her. When she turned to look at him standing among the throng of hippy types and students in Mao jackets, she was surprised to see a tall, slim man, wearing a suit and tie, having perhaps wandered into this crowd from an office job on his lunch break. She smiled at him, and David Simpson stood, rooted like a tree, with a silly grin slowly dawning on his face.

After they'd stood there for awhile like that, Gillian began to feel a bit self-conscious. She started to rummage in her purse for a handkerchief to blot the dampness from her cheeks, and then David was standing right beside her, clearing his throat, asking her whether she would like to go to lunch with him. She looked up at him. He was trembling slightly from nervousness. He seemed sweet and non-threatening, so she said yes, if they could go somewhere close by, since she only had an hour. He seemed surprised that what came out of her mouth was Canadian-accented English, but he didn't withdraw his offer.

They walked together across the park, making slightly stilted small talk. Gillian smoothed things along, asking David his name, where he was from (since he didn't sound like a Londoner) and how he came to be among the crowd at Hyde Park. That's how she learned that he came from a village in Yorkshire, worked at a nearby hospital as an administrator, and that he was an ardent supporter of Socialism. His blue eyes burned and he spoke passionately of his admiration for Mao and "her people," which amused her. She knew her parents would be appalled.

They left Hyde Park for a nearby pub, and had steak and kidney pie, washed down with beer. Gillian was ravenous and claims that David looked shocked at how quickly she ate and how much she put away. David always says he was lost in contemplation of her loveliness. He gave her his phone numbers, on a hospital business card, and saw her to the bus, holding her elbow as she mounted the steps. As the bus pulled away, Gillian looked back at him. He was standing in the street, his tie askew and his hair plastered to his head from the humidity. His arm was raised in the air but he wasn't waving. He looked, she said, as though he were holding on to a strap hanging from the ceiling of an invisible bus, waiting for it to pull away from the curb.

She apologized to the pharmacy student, saying she had got muddled trying to find her way to meet him at the university. He took her out for supper at his father's Chinese restaurant, and introduced the waiter as his older brother. She felt awkward with the student taking her hand over the table and stroking it, continuing even after the food had arrived, and his brother laid it down with a flourish. She noticed how the student's Adam's apple bobbed as he spoke to her, how thin his wrists were, how his shoulders bowed as though under some constant burden. She smiled politely at him and tried to take her hand away but it seemed that body language was not his forte.

Gillian and David saw each other every day for the remaining two weeks she spent in London. Every lunch hour, they would meet at Hyde Park and walk to a nearby restaurant. David knew the ones where the food was good and the service prompt, and he paid the bill every time, except one day when Gillian snatched it from his hands. She shot him a mischievous smile and said, "In Chinese culture, we always fight over the bill—and whoever wins, pays." She paused slightly, then added, "Besides, under the Communists, men and women are equal." David, looking slightly disoriented, acknowledged his defeat—though when the waiter came to him to collect the money, and Gillian held a couple pound notes across the table, he looked pale and squirmed in his chair. David was, from the beginning, ever a gentleman.

On the day before Gillian was to leave for Canada, David asked if they could have a picnic in Hyde Park instead of going to one of the restaurants. She agreed, saying that if he would bring the food, she would bring the wine. They met at a bench on the edge of the park, under a tall elm tree. There was a gentle drizzle coming down, but it was not enough to deter them from eating outside under their umbrellas. David spread a red and white checked table cloth on the bench and from his picnic basket pulled out a brass candlestick holder with a long white taper in it. When he lit it between them, it sizzled with damp and flickered but then held steady.

Gillian ate the sandwiches he brought, enjoying the curious glances from passersby. She had brought the wine in a thermos, and they drank it out of the plastic thermos cup. After they had finished the sandwiches and were on the last of the wine, my mother broke into the Maoist favourite "The East is Red." David, red-faced and earnest, joined in. She started laughing, and he looked at her with soupy eyes full of tenderness. He pulled a small box from his jacket pocket, and flipped it open in front of her.

"Gillian Wong, will you marry me?" he asked. She gaped at him, thunderstruck. He scrambled to recover. "I know it's sudden but you're going back to Canada and I...I want you to stay. I want you to be my wife."

Gillian looked at the ring. It had a slender white gold band and a diamond, with two smaller ones arranged on either side. She looked at David's face. He was leaning toward her, searching her eyes, trying to find her answer in them. She thought of having to tell her Uncle and Aunt, who didn't even know she'd been meeting my father every day. Of the young Chinese pharmacy student, who hung around her like a puppy and wrote her awkward love poems. Of her parents. She covered her mouth with her hand. She felt slightly hysterical.

David's brow furrowed with concern, and confusion. Was she going to cry?

"Gillian. If you need more time…" he said desperately. And Gillian, for once in her life, made the least impetuous, most conservative choice.

"No, David. I don't need more time. I'm so, so sorry…" His face crumpled. "I can't marry you. I hardly know you," she continued. He turned away, the ring box in his limp hand on his lap. "David," she commanded. He looked at her, his eyes rimmed red. "David. We can write. We can visit each other. We can get to know each other better." She reached over to caress his cheek. His eyes melted, and tears sprang up in the corners. At that moment, she knew that she would marry him—but she was going to have to find a way to satisfy her parents, and let the pharmacy student save face.

Gillian caught a plane back to Halifax the next day. She asked David not to see her off, saying she didn't want a tearful farewell. Meek and wounded, he agreed. Aunt and Uncle Wah did accompany her though, and the Chinese student also. While Aunt and Uncle Wah handed her boxes of Chinese pastries tied with string to take back to her parents, the pharmacy student gazed at her, silent and mournful, until it was time for her to check through security. My mother shook his hand, hugged the Wahs, and turned her back on them.

On the plane ride home, Gillian had a window seat, and spent most of the trip gazing out at the cloudscape. It was so alien and bright, and abstract, not at all like the cloud cities of her childhood imaginings. There were no castles, no flying cars, no angels—just a sea of white, over-arced by the eternally blue sky.

David had given her a photo of himself, which she took out of her wallet, somewhere over the North Atlantic. It was his slightly younger self, eyes intensely blue, and dark hair longer than his current haircut. She thought his smile beautiful, eager, full of hope but also ambition. It could be she fell in love with his photo, not with him. She still has that photo to this day—at the bottom of her jewellery box, yellowing with age, the corners curling inward.

Gillian thought of telling the pharmacy student that she was pregnant, but she realized that this story was preposterous—it would make its way back to her parents and would devastate them. The same went for saying she had a pre-existing medical condition and that she couldn't have children. She thought about telling him she didn't want to leave her parents, which was not true—but it might work in a pinch. The pharmacy student, who had come to London via Hong Kong, was not likely to want to settle in Nova Scotia, especially with his own aging parents across the Atlantic. Her parents had resigned themselves to the fact that their only child would go to where her husband's family lived—it was the Chinese way that a daughter became a part of her husband's family. Besides they knew she was restless, that she wanted to see the world—that was one reason they'd sent her to find a husband in England. At least, they thought, life away from Nova Scotia might seem more exotic and hold her interest until she settled down and had children of her own.

Gillian realized that if she was going to tell this story to both the pharmacy student and her parents, she'd also have to tell the same thing to David. She felt quite certain that he would not want to leave London to come to Nova Scotia either—after all, who would? Perhaps they would carry on a "long distance relationship," the sort she had read in a women's magazine was becoming more common. Eventually she would be convinced, with tearful protest, that she must join him in London. Her parents would by then be resigned to the fact that she had a non-Chinese boyfriend, and just be happy to see her married off, she was certain. Gillian closed her eyes and leaned her head against the airplane window, smiling with relief.

Three

When Gillian got off the plane, her parents were there to greet her. Her mother was short and plump with tight black curls and a round face. Her father, tall, thin and slightly stooped, took the pastry boxes from her hands, and wrapped his arms around her in a hug. Her mother pressed her cheek briefly to Gillian's, then launched into the questions.

"So, what he like?" she demanded. "He good student, I know. Is he smart? You like him?" Gillian knew the types of questions her mother would ask, and had been preparing her answers.

"He's a nice guy, Mom. He was a gentleman and showed me around London. We ate in his father's restaurant, which is very nice. He studies hard, so I didn't spend as much time with him as I would have liked."

Mrs. Wong folded her arms across her chest. "You no like him," she said. Her daughter shrugged noncommittally. "You no like a good Chinese boy, who study pharmacy and want to be someone. Why you no like him?"

Mr. Wong, who was never comfortable with conflict, waved his hand as if to erase something in the air, but his wife stood still and refused to budge till Gillian had answered. Gillian was forced to roll out her prize excuse earlier than she had planned. She took a deep breath and prepared to plead for her life.

"Ma, he lives so far away. I don't want to be that far away

from you and Daddy. You're not getting any younger, you know, and I want to be around to help take care of you."

Mr. Wong beamed, and turned to his wife. "You see what a good daughter we have?" he proclaimed, putting his arm around Gillian's shoulders and squeezing her to him. Mrs. Wong looked at her daughter through narrowed eyes, and said nothing.

When they got home, they sat at the kitchen table and spread the pastry boxes over its scuffed Formica surface. Mr. Wong, who loved Chinese baked goods, immediately started on an egg custard tart, while Mrs. Wong helped herself to a bun with red bean paste. She sat back in her chair, her hand around her tea cup. Gillian talked about seeing Big Ben and the changing of the guard at Buckingham Palace; of Madame Tussaud's Wax Museum, where she had her photograph taken with Elvis and Hitler, and the Tower of London where huge ravens were watched over by men dressed as Beefeaters.

Mrs. Wong listened with a severe look on her face. Gillian could tell her mother was thinking, turning everything over in her mind, and it made her nervous. Suddenly, Mrs. Wong opened with another tack.

"You enjoy your trip. We pay a lot of money for you to go to London to find husband." Mr. Wong closed his eyes and shook his head. Gillian looked down at her tea.

"I know Ma. It was nice to go away but I felt homesick. I wanted to be here with you."

But her mother wasn't buying it. "This Chinese boy like you very much. Your Aunt Pearl tell me he like a puppy dog—love sick. He miss you already." Gillian covered her face with her hands. Her father threw his hands into the air, weakly, and went to the living room to sit in his chair and read the Chinese paper Gillian had brought him from London.

Gillian was no match for her mother, and she knew it. But

she felt stubborn and defiant, and decided her best tactic was to keep silent. Mrs. Wong recognized that approach. She got up, stiffly, her daughter noticed, and brought a colander of beans to the table. She began to pinch off their tops and tails to prepare them for cooking. Gillian picked up a bean and did the same.

"London is a great city," Mrs. Wong said, as though she had spent some time musing on the cultural capitals of the world. "Many different kind of people there. Black, Jew, Arab. Lots of Chinese. You meet any other Chinese boys?" she asked.

Gillian sighed and nodded. "Auntie took me around to meet her friends. There were some Chinese boys."

Mrs. Wong softened a little. "So? You like any?" she asked in a conversational tone. Gillian shook her head. She knew she was going to have to tell her mother about David sooner or later and she was suddenly feeling too tired to fight. She opened her purse, took out my father's picture, and handed it to her mother.

Mrs. Wong took the half-glasses that dangled from a chain around her neck and peered down at the small snapshot in her hands. Gillian watched her mother's mouth harden, and her heart sank. Then something happened that surprised her. Her mother expelled a long sigh as if she had been holding her breath for a long time, and wiped a tear from her eye. She looked suddenly very old. Gillian took her hand. Her mother said, "Ai-ya. Don't tell your father. He no understand."

Mrs. Wong broke the news to her husband that night, as they were going to bed. Gillian, from her room beside theirs, heard her father exclaim "Ai-ya." There was a hushed, rapid-fire exchange in Chinese. Gillian pictured her father sitting up in bed, holding his head. Sometime later her parents' bedroom door opened and she heard her father go downstairs. After a few minutes, Gillian quietly made her way down the stairs to the kitchen door. Her father was sitting in the dark at the kitchen table smoking a cigarette. The light from the street lamp bathed his face and naked torso, throwing sharp shadows from his nose and collarbones. She stood in the doorway, watching him but he never turned to look at her. Eventually, her heart aching, she made her way back to bed.

Under the watchful eye of her mother, Gillian wrote a letter to the pharmacy student. It sounded tearful and apologetic. She was writing with great regret to tell the student that she was honoured to have met him but that upon coming home, she realized she could not part from her dear mother and father. That London was too far away, that her heart would break if she had to leave them. That she was sorry for giving him hope, but that she was sure that he would find a wonderful wife because of his upright character and devotion to his studies, and his undoubted future professional success. Mrs. Wong was satisfied. She licked the envelope and tucked it into her apron pocket to mail.

I know my mother still thinks about what life would have been like, had she not walked into Hyde Park the day she met my father. Hands around a cup of tea at the kitchen table, she gazes out the window, as if she were looking into another world. She wonders whether she would have been happier with the Chinese student, living in London, where she could have felt the pulse of the world, instead of in this small town where her life has slowly dripped away, like a faucet not quite turned off. She weighs things in her mind, as though with an old-fashioned scale—a thimbleful of this, an ounce of that—the things she chose and those she left behind. It never seems as if she comes to any resolution— she still doesn't know if she made the best possible choice. She drinks her cup of tea to the bottom, gets up slowly from her chair, and wipes her hands on her apron or her slacks, as though to say, "Well, that's that, then."

Four

But she had gone to Hyde Park, and she had met my father. And so Gillian and David began a feverish cross-Atlantic correspondence. David also called her every Sunday at precisely three p.m. They arranged it this way so that her father would know not to pick up the phone—it would save him the unpleasantness of speaking to David. Gillian would be sitting at the kitchen table, filing her nails. She jumped when the phone rang, even though she knew it would ring, even though David never missed calling her, not even once. Mr. Wong would be sitting in the living room, reading the paper and pretending to be deaf while Mrs. Wong, fiercely crocheting another doily, would from time to time glance toward the kitchen when she heard her daughter giggle.

After several months of this, it was arranged. David would fly to Nova Scotia to meet Gillian's family. She didn't dare ask that he stay at her parents' house. Instead, he would stay at a rooming house downtown. Gillian didn't have the heart to tell him how the odds of him being accepted by her parents were stacked against him. He was blissfully ignorant, excited only at the thought of seeing her again. The few nights before he arrived, Gillian cried in bed from apprehension and anxiety, and woke up exhausted. But she was also happy, almost breathless, and she hardly cared about her parents' grim looks and stoic silences.

David arrived in a drizzle of rain. Mr. Wong and Gillian drove to pick him up at the airport. When he emerged from the overseas arrival entrance, Gillian clapped her hands to her cheeks and squealed, the way young women did at a Beatles concert. David looked bewildered, tired and pleased—he encircled her with his arms and kissed the top of her head. Mr. Wong stood back from them, smoking a cigarette. David put his small carry-on case down on the ground and extended his hand to shake Gillian's father's. Mr. Wong hesitated, but politeness won out. He briefly took David's hand and grimaced in place of a smile.

Mrs. Wong was waiting at home. Hearing that David liked Chinese food, she had offered to cook a Chinese meal for him before he went to the rooming house. Looking prim in her spotless apron and pearl earrings, she smiled briefly at David and ushered everyone into the dining room. Gillian was the first to realize something was amiss. She sat down next to my father and looked at the table.

There was the roast duck, with its head still intact, its bill pointing to where my father sat. Chicken feet clawed the air from a bowl next to his plate. The white eyeball of a steamed fish stared blindly up at the ceiling. Mrs. Wong was trying to frighten her guest off with food.

She pushed the roast duck toward him. "You take head, brains are very good," she told David. She also served him the fish head and a few chicken feet. Gillian looked aghast. "Heads and feet are very nutritious," her mother continued.

David looked down at his plate, mouth gaping slightly. But he was ravenous and game to try anything, particularly to please Gillian's parents. He picked up the duck head and cracked it open with his hands. Then he slurped the insides, as he had seen an old man do at a Chinese restaurant he frequented. Mrs. Wong, a spoonful of soup halfway to her mouth, gawked in surprise. David picked the fish head up with his chop sticks and sucked the flesh off it, including the eyeball. The difficult work out of the way, he turned with gusto to the chicken feet.

"I love these," he said, "but usually they're only served at dim sum, aren't they?" With appreciative noises, he sucked the spicy sauce off the rubbery claws, dislocating the small bones and plucking them expertly from his mouth one at a time with his chop sticks.

Mr. Wong's face was shiny with surprise, his eyebrows arched toward the ceiling. He put his head down and spooned up mouthful after mouthful of soup. But his shoulders were shaking and eventually he excused himself. In the living room he blew his nose several times and returned to the table, where-upon he sat down in dignified silence and used his chopsticks to put the choicest portions of duck, fish and vegetables into David's bowl of rice. Still hungry, David downed everything gratefully while Gillian's mother looked on with lips pursed.

At the end of the meal, Mrs. Wong served tea and oranges. David pushed his chair away from the table and burped, which he knew was the Chinese way to show appreciation to the cook after a good meal. As Mrs. Wong poured him tea, David touched her sleeve.

"That was a fabulous meal," he pronounced. "In fact, that was the best Chinese food I have ever tasted," he added. Mrs. Wong's eyes softened and her mouth loosened. He didn't know it but David had sent a gentle arrow directly to her heart.

Gillian could see how things were turning out, how her mother's ploy had turned in on itself. In Gillian's face there was pain, sharp and sweet. David thought she looked lovelier than at any other time he'd seen her. He held her hand under the table.

After supper David felt suddenly exhausted—from the flight and the anticipation of seeing his love and from knowing he had passed some kind of test. He sat on the sofa, longing to hold Gillian in his arms. But Mr. Wong was watching television and the flicker and hum of the evening news lulled him to sleep so that finally his head fell back and his mouth fell open in a loud snore. Gillian put her hand to her mouth to stifle a giggle. Her mother looked severe for a moment, as though she were struggling with her own face, and finally she smiled a prim smile.

"He okay, this boyfriend. Better if he Chinese, but he okay."

Later, when David woke up, Gillian and Mr. Wong drove him to the rooming house. It was a slightly shabby old building, its clapboard siding painted grey, but a welcoming light shone over the front door. While Mr. Wong stayed in the car, smoking a cigarette, David and Gillian were able to talk to one another in semi-privacy for the first time. David stroked her cheek, and she looked up at him with eyes shining. He kissed her softly on the mouth, and pressed a little box into her hand. Then he turned to wave at Mr. Wong and stepped out of the light, through the front door of the rooming house.

Gillian felt immediately bereft. Mr. Wong got out and gently steered her back to the car.

"Ai-ya, don't cry," he said, wiping a tear from her cheek with the back of his hand. "You see him tomorrow. Tomorrow is not so far away."

Gillian buried her face in her hands. It was not just because she had to leave her love at the rooming house that she cried, but that, after being separated from her by an ocean, he had managed somehow to walk over the equally wide ocean of her parents' disapproval. It was wholly unexpected, and Gillian, who had been ready to put up a valiant fight, felt both relief and disappointment. If her tears could have been analyzed, the scientists would have been curious about the strange mixture of happiness and sadness, frustration and fulfillment.

They would have been both salty and sweet.

When she went to bed that night, Gillian opened the box my father had given her. She was filled with eager anticipation and also fear, that it might be another ring—but surely he would have given it to her when they were alone together, where he could see the expression on her face. But it wasn't a ring—it was a tiny, blown glass bird. A pigeon or a dove, something David had picked up in a shop in London's Chinatown. Gillian held it in the flat of her hand, under her reading lamp. It perched there, as though in a nest, among the intersecting lines of her palm. It was beautiful, she thought, but useless—for what could she do with it? How could she even display it? And then she realized that it was meant for her alone, a talisman of his love. He was like Noah, sending out a dove to reach land after the flood and finding her.

David stayed in Nova Scotia for two weeks. Mr. Wong drove him and Gillian to Peggy's Cove, where David marvelled over the sparkling white granite and enjoyed a lobster dinner. They also went to the Annapolis Valley, and picked strawberries. David closed his eyes to remember the smell of the berries baking in the sun, and the vision of Gillian holding on to her sun hat while she bent over the plants.

But what he loved best was the ocean and walking along the beach holding Gillian's hand, while her parents followed at a discreet distance. He loved the way the sun sparked off his bare feet as he walked along the wet sand, and the sound of the waves washing back through the pebbles that lined the beach. The dogs dripping and chasing after sticks, the little plovers with their skinny legs racing zigzag after the tide to eat whatever little creatures were left behind. He loved the salty wind and the way Gillian's dark hair whipped and snaked, medusa-like. And the way her forehead relaxed, and her eyes took on a far-off, dreamy look as she gazed out at the empty horizon.

On his last day before he was to return to England, the two of them walked arm in arm along the beach, while the Wongs went to the nearby restaurant. Gillian was pale and quiet, and David, lost in his own thoughts. They found a washed up log to sit down on, huddled together in their trench coats. It was overcast, and windy and there were few swimmers that day.

David had rehearsed what he was going to say, ever since she had refused him that day on the bench.

"You know, Gillian, ever since I met you, I thought you were the kind of person who could sense other peoples' thoughts. Sometimes I thought you were laughing at me for the things that went through my mind." Gillian looked hurt and shook her head. "No?" David asked, pleased. "I had the feeling that if I closed my eyes and asked you a question in my head, you would be able to hear it and answer me. Let me know if you can hear what I'm saying."

Gillian looked up at him, slightly incredulous. He closed his eyes and a serene expression came over his face. Gillian held his hand and looked out at the sea. Then her eyes widened and she leapt to her feet, scattering sand everywhere.

"Will you marry me? Is that what you're asking?" she cried.

David smiled and held out his hand to her. "Yes, that's what I was asking and yes, I'll marry you, if you like."

Gillian was not telepathic—David had merely invented that idea. He was afraid to ask her to marry him once more, in case she refused him and broke his heart for the second time. So he decided that he would leave the matter to her, knowing that she would hear him say whatever was in her own heart. If she had thought she'd heard him say "the beach is lovely," he would have smiled and agreed. If she'd said she'd heard him say "I am tired of Gillian Wong and I want to go home," he would have protested and comforted her, telling her he was mistaken about her telepathic abilities. But she had heard him say exactly what he had hoped. That was, of course, in the first days of their courtship before their hearts became deaf to one another. Before they were like two fish swimming in tanks side by side—they could see one another but, for all intents and purposes, inhabited separate oceans.

Five

David went back to England the next day, but they agreed that he and Gillian would get married at the first possible opportunity. They knew their families would not approve of a hasty decision, so they considered eloping. Gillian thought this was an exciting prospect—she pictured herself and David on a ship in the middle of the Atlantic, being married by the captain in a swirl of fog. David was for once the less romantic and more practical one. He thought they should arrange for a justice of the peace to marry them, and also that he should begin applying for jobs in Nova Scotia. Gillian was crestfallen about the idea of not living in London, and argued her case with David, but considering her letter to the pharmacy student, she realized that she probably couldn't make such a quick appearance in London with a new husband. Still, she decided she would make the trip to England to meet her future in-laws, and hoped that she would convince David to elope there.

A few months after David returned to London, Gillian was on a plane to see him. This time it was David who paid for her flight, a generous gesture that pleased my grandparents. Gillian was ostensibly to stay in a hotel near his flat, but in fact she stayed there only one night. After that, she coaxed David into allowing her to sleep on his sofa, and while he was snoring, she came to the door of his bedroom in her white nightgown. He awoke to find her giggling with her hand over her mouth.

Then she tucked herself under his covers, and put her cold feet on his. He trembled, his teeth chattering, and buried his face in her hair.

The next day, they eloped. David, bedazzled, let my mother drag him to city hall to be married by a justice of the peace. His friend George, husky, red-faced and yawning, and a co-worker who was there long enough to sign his name and then was gone, stood as witnesses. Afterwards, the happy couple and George celebrated in the pub across the street. After half a pint of beer Gillian kissed George on the cheek as a thank-you, which made him blush an even deeper red. David leaned back in his chair, gazing at his new wife with a pleasant satiety and undisguised adoration. And Gillian, who liked to be the centre of attention, was radiant—she had reached two pinnacles of womanhood in fewer than twenty-four hours, and was as excited as a child at Christmas.

Actually, Gillian had reached three pinnacles of woman-hood—she was pregnant and blissfully unaware—even though her nerves shook with happiness at the queasy unreal-ity of it all, and her body closed like cupped hands around me in her womb, to protect me from worldly disappointments.

That afternoon, David and Gillian drove to York, where his parents still lived in a little brick row house with a rose garden out front. He had telephoned them to say he was coming home to visit, and that he was bringing his new wife. Gillian looked up at him anxiously as he twisted the phone cord in his hand, wondering how they would react. She was surprised that David's face was almost expressionless, that his voice remained low and conversational. When he put down the phone, he tried to smile.

"My parents would like to meet you," he said. Gillian stared at him. "They said that they are pleased I am married and won't we come home?" He looked ashen. David had rarely been able to do anything that would disturb his parents' equanimity, and for their part, they had become resigned to the fact that he would always try.

But Gillian turned out to be a bigger surprise than they'd imagined. When the newly married couple reached David's family home in the little village of Haxby, his father was digging at the earth near the front door, where gardens would be planted, while his mother stood on the steps to welcome them. When she saw Gillian, Mrs. Simpson's soft and pleasant face took on a baffled expression.

"William, they're here," she called out. Mr. Simpson straightened up to greet them. When he saw his daughter-in-law, he blushed from confusion. Gillian could tell right away that they were shocked that she wasn't Caucasian, that her husband hadn't told them otherwise. She had thought the big news would be that they'd eloped, not that she was Chinese. She was mortified.

"Mum, Dad—this is Gillian. My new wife," David said, his voice shaking slightly.

His father took off his work gloves to shake Gillian's hand, while Mrs. Simpson ushered them into the house, and then went into the kitchen to make tea. Mr. Simpson sat down in his chair in a corner of the little front sitting room and lit his pipe. Gillian sat straight-backed on the edge of the sofa, and David stood with his hand on her shoulder. He was clearly flustered and nervous, talking into the air about Gillian coming all the way from Nova Scotia and what a long flight it was, but she didn't once turn her head to look at him. She stared straight ahead.

Finally Mr. Simpson cleared his throat. "So...you're from Canada?" he asked, as if he hadn't heard anything David had said. Gillian nodded and smiled a tight little smile. Mr. Simpson took an atlas down from the bookshelf next to him.

He searched for a moment to find the page with the map of Canada, then handed it to Gillian.

"Which part?" he inquired. She pointed to Nova Scotia. Mr. Simpson sat back, looking pleased. "Why, I didn't know there were Eskimos that far south."

Gillian's mouth fell open. David pulled his hand over his face, as though pulling a cobweb off it. In a thin voice, with mounting hysteria, he said, "No, Dad, Gillian isn't an Eskimo. Her parents are from China, but they're all Canadian now."

Mr. Simpson peered at Gillian's face. "Well yes...I can see that now," he said in a jovial voice. "Canada is full of all sorts, a bit like England." He leaned back and held his hands over his stomach. David stroked his wife's shoulder nervously.

"When did your parents go to Canada then? Were they escaping from the Communists and Mao's armies?" David groaned, and his father looked up at him good-naturedly and shrugged.

But Gillian saw her chance to drive a nail into her husband's heart. "Well, yes they were. In fact they left behind their house and all their belongings, before the Communists came to their village. They were against Mao from the start." David's face was ashen. Mr. Simpson nodded his approval.

"Communists," he said, "are the scourge of the earth. They'll take everything a man has earned by the sweat of his brow and hand it over to some lazy sod who never worked a day, but can shout slogans."

Mrs. Simpson came out of the kitchen wiping her hands on a dish towel. She had a brave look that said she'd been through the war and she could get through this.

"Would you like Chinese tea then?" she asked Gillian. "We have some jasmine leftover from when David lived here. I'm sure it's still good." Gillian, who looked as though she had just sucked in a breath of sharp mountain air, shook her head.

"No thank you. Regular tea will be fine."

David, looking miserable, sat down next to his wife. She didn't look at him. Her hands were clasped between her knees, which stuck (demurely) out from under her mini dress. Mrs. Simpson sat down opposite her, settling plumply into the chair and placing the tray between them. She looked slightly bewildered as though she was trying to decide which smile to use. Gillian didn't smile at all—she was stiff but shell-shocked. Why wouldn't he have told his parents that she was Chinese? Was he ashamed of her? She felt warm tears beginning to seep up over the rims of her eyes, as though they were pots ready to boil over. But Gillian was proud and stopped the tears by hardening her heart.

Mr. Simpson sat back in his seat and started to read the paper, puffing on his pipe. Just like my father, Gillian thought. Not that it made her feel any better. In fact, sitting in this little council house with David's parents, she felt as though they had somehow shrunk to fit into the tiny rooms, so different from the open plan of her parents' living-dining room. And it seemed as though the walls were closing in on her. The pressure of David's hand on her shoulder, which seemed to be pushing her down into her seat, was almost unbearable.

Gillian stood up suddenly. "Can I use your bathroom?" she blurted. Mr. Simpson looked up from his paper and chuckled.

"Ah, you Americans," he said. "You mean the lavatory, the WC. A Yorkshireman's invention, by the way." Gillian looked confused. Mr. Simpson pointed with his pipe to the stairs. "Upstairs on your left."

David sat down at the table, his head in his hand. When Gillian had gone upstairs, Mr. Simpson put down his paper and looked at his son. He chewed on the end of his pipe, deliberating.

"Well, she's a bonny lass," Mr. Simpson said after a bit.

Mrs. Simpson's brow uncreased. "Yes David," she said, putting her soft hand on her son's. "But you should have told us."

Gillian stood looking at herself in the bathroom mirror. Her nose was red, and the rims of her eyes, as though she were coming down with a cold. She was angry and anguished, but she wouldn't cry, even though it felt as though spears were cutting through her. It wasn't clear to her what she should do, and her head felt as though it were stuffed with cotton batten. She sat on the toilet seat, with her head in her hands and her heart aching.

Someone was knocking on the door. Gillian grabbed some toilet paper from the roll and flushed the toilet.

"Just a minute," she said. She splashed some cold water from the tap on her face and wiped it on the guest towel. Then she took a quavery breath and opened the door

Mrs. Simpson stood there with a face cloth, bath towel and some bath salts. She smiled apologetically and laid them on the counter.

"You've come such a long way, dear, I thought perhaps you'd like a hot bath and a good rest." Gillian stared down at the offering. "Don't mind David, dear," said his mother with a gentle pat of her hand. "He's a good boy. He would never hurt anyone on purpose." Then she let out a little sigh and turned stiffly. Her legs were slightly bowed and her shoulders tipped from side to side as she took each step. Gillian imagined her own grandmother's bound feet, curled tiny as fists in their little slippers. She would have been about the age of David's mother, were she still alive.

Gillian ran a bath. The pipes clanked and groaned, but eventually there was enough water in the old clawfoot tub for her to lie down in. She stepped out of her clothes and put her foot into the water. It struck her that this act of stepping naked into a strange bathtub meant she was saying yes to something.

Yes to David's parents and their awkwardness. Yes to David, who hadn't had the courage to tell them he was in love with her, a Chinese-Canadian girl. Yes to a life which she saw now would involve certain kinds of compromise and perhaps unhappiness. But because she loved David and because she couldn't see another path for herself, she stepped into the tub and slipped down into the water. Tears seeped out of her eyes but she brushed them away—as though they were ticklish feathers that had somehow escaped from the down quilt of the water that covered her.

Later, when they were going to bed in the little spare room, decorated with wallpaper covered in tea roses, David explained to her that his parents were of a generation that would find a Chinese daughter-in-law difficult to accept. All his other girlfriends had been white English girls, and *naturally* they expected him to marry someone of his own race. David stammered nervously as he said this and stroked her hand. He should have told them, he admitted. He should have prepared them. He shouldn't have put her in such an awkward position. His parents had never understood his fascination with China and it seemed better to just introduce her as a *fait accompli*, instead of going through all the difficult explanations. Gillian listened and nodded. Though timid in the face of her silence, my father was almost grateful that she said nothing.

They spent a week driving in the countryside. David showed his new wife the various places from his youth—the house where he was born, the first school he attended. The factory where his father had worked. They all looked, to Gillian, past their heyday. And to David, everything seemed so small. The roads he had bicycled as a child were mere paths and could be traversed in a minute by car. There were houses creeping on to the fields where he used to catch crickets and the stream he played in was merely a trickle running through a culvert now. David seemed crestfallen, Gillian thought. He had wanted to show her something of what he remembered as his idyllic childhood, and it had been taken away from him by progress.

Gillian wasn't interested in David's past. She felt as though he were trying to convince her of something she didn't believe in. Her flight from her own childhood and its pains and boredoms were too recent, too fresh. It was only five years ago that her best childhood friend joined forces with a group of girls who shunned her, and only three since a boy who she had secretly loved had got a schoolmate pregnant. Gillian was hungry to escape the miserable bondage of childhood—she wanted only the future, as spotted and imperfect as it might turn out to be.

Gillian flew home, leaving David to go back to his job in London. She brought with her in her suitcase a letter of introduction, outlining his experience and qualifications, to mail to the hospital in Halifax. Gillian had quietly resigned her hopes that she might end up living in London after all. And she felt the tug of her parents, as strong as the moon on the tide, pulling her home. This was something she had not expected, something that perhaps came with her recent disappointments. David was not an anchor, but a boat, adrift on the same sea as she was.

Six

Before Gillian's plane landed, she slipped off her wedding band and put it in her pocket. She wasn't sure how she would tell her parents she had eloped, and on the plane ride home her mind had been otherwise occupied. So the easiest thing, she thought, would be to keep quiet until the time seemed right.

Her parents were waiting for her, near the back of the crowd of people milling around to welcome the international travellers. Mrs. Wong looked very small, and Mr. Wong very tall and thin next to her. Their faces lit up when they saw her and they hurried toward her. A rush of feeling—happiness, homesickness, regret—washed through her.

Mrs. Wong held Gillian by the elbow and patted her arm, while Mr. Wong hugged her with his arm around her shoulders. He then went to watch for Gillian's suitcase to come around on the luggage carousel.

Gillian and her mother went to sit down on a bench to wait. Mrs. Wong took a package of pink wafer cookies out of her purse, and a couple of cans of 7-Up. She never bought food out if she could bring something from home. Gillian, who usually felt embarrassed by the larder her mother carried around in her purse, slurped her can of pop gratefully.

Mrs. Wong looked at her. Gillian's cheeks were glowing, and her hair and eyes looked shiny. There was something different about her daughter, something that tugged at her heart like a child tugs at its mother's hand. Mrs. Wong's eyes opened wide and she put her hand to her lips. In Chinese she whispered, "Are you pregnant?"

Gillian choked on her pop. Could that be why she was feeling queasy? She put her hand over her belly protectively. Her mother grasped her wrist in an iron grip.

"Gillian, I hope you no do something stupid." She looked at her daughter through narrowed eyes, searching for an answer. Gillian put her left hand in her pocket and slipped the ring on her finger. With a meek smile, she presented it for her mother's inspection.

Mrs. Wong's face softened and her small mouth began to tremble. "Ai-ya," she said, "You marry without your parents." She pulled a handkerchief from her purse and blew her nose. "Your father wanted to walk with you down the aisle. Why you do this to us?"

Gillian felt a sting in her heart. She realized that she had been selfish. It had never occurred to her that her mother was anything but dictatorial and a nag and that her father was old-fashioned. Now she saw that she had been thinking of no one but herself when she eloped with David. Tears began to seep out of her eye corners. She grasped her mother's hands.

"I'm sorry Ma," she murmured.

Mr. Wong came up to them with the suitcase in his hand. When he saw them crying, he put the suitcase down, bewildered. Mrs. Wong waved her tears away with her handkerchief and held out her daughter's left hand. Mr. Wong's jaw dropped, and his face became, to Gillian's eyes, unreadable. Without saying anything, he took her by the arm and led her out to the car, my grandmother hurrying behind them.

During the drive home, the car was full of a woolly silence. Gillian looked out the window, so she wouldn't have to gaze at the back of her parents' heads. When they were nearing the city, at a four-way stop, Mr. Wong slammed on the brakes and hit his palm on the dashboard. He started swearing in Chinese, while his wife tried to calm him in hushed tones.

Gillian covered her ears, hunched down in the seat and began to cry. Mrs. Wong had had enough. Her small plump hand shot out to prevent her husband from hitting the dashboard again.

"She is pregnant," Mrs. Wong hissed. "It is better she is married now. We should be happy." Mr. Wong's eyebrows shot up. Mrs. Wong rubbed his shoulders. "We must be happy," she said fiercely. "We will have a grandchild."

Mr. Wong said nothing. He got out of the car, and began to walk toward town.

Mrs. Wong didn't know how to drive, so Gillian, weeping, climbed behind the steering wheel. She headed into town, slowly passing her father who was walking on the opposite shoulder. He didn't look at her when she rolled down the window and said "Pa, please." There was no traffic so she drove slowly alongside him. Mrs. Wong spoke to her husband in rapid-fire Chinese, angry and pleading. But he kept on walking. Defeated she told her daughter, "Drive. Your father is a stubborn old man. Let him walk."

It was two miles to their house. Gillian drove past her father and gradually sped up until he was a mere speck in her rear-view mirror. A few large flakes of snow began to fall. When they reached home she turned to look for him on the road but of course he was too far away to be seen. Mrs. Wong walked with quick steps to the front door, without turning to look behind her. Gillian followed more slowly. It was strange to come home; though she was married and if her mother was right, pregnant, she still felt like a child. She would always be a child as long as she lived in this house.

Gillian sat by the living room window, drinking tea. Her father appeared half an hour later, walking stiffly up the driveway, his hair plastered to his head and his face moist. She wasn't able to tell if he had been crying. He looked calm, almost serene. She stood up and went to her room, so that he would not have to talk to her, be reminded of her reckless disregard for her parents' feelings.

She lay on her bed, under the same faded comforter she'd had since she was seven. Her stuffed animals, looking slightly ragged, lined a shelf above her. The wallpaper was pink and flowery, peeling slightly in places, and the ceiling was cracked. She had often fantasized that something would come through that crack, the roots of a tree, or perhaps something sinister, a troll or an ogre; sometimes she imagined it was the hooves of a white horse bearing a prince that had created the crack—that he would come crashing down and scoop her up in his arms. But today it was just a crack. As she looked up at it, she felt something inside her give way, a firmness in her chest that seemed to collapse under its own weight.

Gillian dozed off in the semi-dark. There was a soft knock on her door but she didn't hear it. Mr. Wong opened the door and stood there, gazing down at her, his only child, now carrying his grandchild. He had been furious when he got out of the car and started walking, angry enough that he could have just kept going, out of the lives of the only two people left in the world that he cared for. One of them was his outrageously disobedient, disrespectful, selfish child. So far she had done nothing but displease her parents, not like a good daughter. He felt an ache of disappointment, that this unruly woman-child didn't think of how her careless actions affected her parents.

As he had walked stiffly along the gravel shoulder of the highway, his anger petered out. The snow, in big soft flakes, fell gently against his face. He blinked, but they clung to his eyelashes momentarily, before melting and dripping down his cheeks. He thought of how he had never wanted anything more than to see his daughter happily married and producing grandchildren. And he stopped short when he realized that she was already fulfilling this dream of his, though not in the way he'd imagined. A sheepish grin slowly dawned on his face. She was always one step ahead of her parents, this daughter of his.

Mr. Wong stood in the doorway watching my mother as she slept. She was hugging one of the ragged teddy bears from her childhood, and her cheeks were flushed from crying. He thought of the times he had tried to read her a bedtime story and she, with the impatience of childhood, would pull the book from his hands, turning the pages herself. She would "read" each page in her own words, having learned it by heart from previous evenings, and when it came to the end, she would announce the conclusion with a dramatic flourish, her eyes wide and shining. Triumphant. As though she'd thought of it herself.

Seven

When Gillian woke up, she stiffened immediately. Something bad had happened—what was it? And then she remembered how her parents had reacted to finding out she was married and pregnant. She put her hand on her belly. It was quite flat. But there was something—her fingertips tingled as she gently massaged her abdomen. Inside her, something as small as a dust mote was dividing over and over. Budding. Flowering.

She sat up slowly, and put a blanket around her shoulders. Her stomach made a gurgling noise. It was almost suppertime. David would be sleeping now in London, his dark curls mashed against the pillow where her own scent still lingered. She thought of him dispassionately, as though he were a stranger. His shoulder blades under the sheet. His bony knees. His boyish enthusiasm for causes, his infatuation with her oriental features, the way he faltered when he brought her before his parents. Dissatisfaction stirred faintly inside her, like a wisp of mist rising from a lake in early morning.

Gillian stood up and put a sweater on. She clutched her arms to her chest, against the coolness of her parents' house and to protect her from what they would say to her. She found them in the kitchen, her father with his hands around a mug of tea, her mother speaking earnestly and quietly as she peeled and sliced an onion for supper. Her father nodded, resigned, and looked up at his daughter in the doorway. Mrs. Wong stopped chopping the onion and turned to face the door. Unsmilingly, she motioned for Gillian to take a chair.

For a while no one spoke. Mr. Wong sipped his tea and stared ahead of him. Mrs. Wong pushed a small wooden chopping board in Gillian's direction and gave her a cleaver to crush and peel some garlic. This ordinary gesture gave Gillian some relief. Her features relaxed as she removed a clove of garlic from its cluster, and with the flat of the cleaver's blade, pounded it so it split its papery skin and the sharp tang of garlic tingled in the air.

Gillian glanced at her father. There was something sheepish in his resignation, as though he were slightly embarrassed. She didn't notice the stone of her mother's face as she chopped up the last onion. Gillian pulled the crushed meat of the garlic from its sticky skin and chopped it into tiny pieces with the cleaver.

Her mother turned to the sink. "You will have a Chinese wedding," she said, without looking up. Gillian stopped chopping and her mouth fell open. Her mother rinsed her hands of the onion under a stream of cold water. "It must be soon—before your belly is round." Gillian put her hand on her abdomen.

"But...but I'm already married. And David can't come here," she stammered. "He paid for my ticket to England, and he won't be able to afford to come here so soon."

Mrs. Wong opened the fridge and bent to take out some coriander. "Doesn't matter," she said, her voice slightly muffled. "No need David." Gillian had a stricken look. Her father cleared his throat and took a sip of tea.

Mrs. Wong straightened up and turned around, her face flushed. She shook the bunch of coriander at her daughter. "You have—how you say—substitute. A substitute husband. Like substitute teacher."

Gillian sat down in the chair across from her father. He

looked down at his cup. He didn't look angry. Her mind ground to a halt. What was her mother saying?

"You wear a beautiful dress. Red and gold. We have a banquet for you, invite Chinese friends. We give lucky money. You have substitute husband. Some your friend, maybe Harold from school." Gillian looked at her uncomprehending. "Oh, we tell everyone you marry in England already. David's parents so old, they no can come to Nova Scotia, and you show them respect—you marry there. We say David, he...he break his leg and no can come to his other wedding—so you have substitute." Mrs. Wong's mouth puckered, her eyes shining fiercely.

Gillian's brain began to churn. This was her mother's revenge, to shame her in the guise of celebration, she thought. She looked at her father, who smiled weakly but kindly back at her.

Mrs. Wong started to chop the coriander violently with the cleaver. Tears began to spring from the corners of her eyes.

"We save face," she said. She rubbed the back of her hand across her brow. Mr. Wong reached across the table and held her hand. She sat down violently, as though she'd been knocked off her feet, and began to sob uncontrollably, hiding her face in her hands.

Gillian realized then what she had done to her parents, what she had been doing her whole life. She had eagerly pursued her own ends—innocently enough, yes, but with such disregard for what her parents were, for the frailty of their world here in this country where they remained foreigners. She had wanted only to be a white girl, had shrunk from being Chinese as though it were some rotting fruit, as though it weren't even a part of her. She had listened to Western music, dressed like Western girls, lusted after Western boys—and finally married a man who, for all his Sinophilia, knew nothing about what it meant to be Chinese.

But the worst of it, she realized, was this. She hadn't let them share her wedding day. It had seemed much cleaner and simpler somehow to marry as she had—to elope, to have it over and done with, so that no one—not even she—could change their minds. She realized that she'd somehow dreaded the wedding—all the preparations and arrangements that most brides revel in—that would culminate with herself standing there with David with their parents on either side of them. The unreality of that conclusion made her panic—as though if she didn't force the issue, it wouldn't happen at all. So to circumnavigate the impossibility of the situation, she had rushed forward, pushing against the boundaries of what was seemly, respectful and orderly. She left her parents in her wake as usual, clinging to one another for dear life.

"Ma..." she whispered. "Ma...don't cry." She stretched out her hand to her mother's head. She noticed how thin Mrs. Wong's hair was, how the little puffs of perm curled around a small bald spot. "Ma?" she asked. Her mother looked up at her through her tears. "Can I have my Chinese wedding at the Anglican church?" Mrs. Wong smiled and snuffled, wiping her nose on a cloth hankie that she'd stuffed up her sleeve.

Eight

It turned out Gillian couldn't have her wedding at the Anglican church, even though the minister knew her—her best friend in grade school had invited her to come to church with her some summer Sundays. Gillian had felt very awkward in Sunday school, where the children sat in a semi-circle around Mrs. Dawes, the minister's wife and the Sunday school teacher, as she scratched out the Word of God on a chalkboard. Although Gillian had read some Bible stories out of a children's picture book at the doctor's office, she was unfamiliar with most of what was being discussed, and it fascinated her. She liked the Old Testament stories best—Adam and Eve, Sampson and Delilah, Jacob and the coat of many colours. Noah's Ark. Jesus and his miracles, unfortunately, left her cold.

Gillian also liked the high ceiling of the sanctuary, and watching the white ceiling fans spin as women fanned themselves with the church program. It was almost as if mechanical angels were hovering overhead, pouring down blessings upon them. And she liked the singing—it was soulful and heartfelt, she thought, and the sound of it rose toward heaven like a stand of fir trees.

The minister, Reverend Dawes, was an old man now, with a bald pate but the same shiny blue eyes. When Gillian came to see him in the rectory, he looked up from the sermon he was writing, peering at her over the tops of his glasses. He smiled at her, recognizing her as the small Chinese girl who had never become a regular parishioner but for whom there was always hope.

Gillian wasn't sure exactly how to ask what she had to, so she began by saying, "Reverend, I was wondering if you would allow me to be married in your church?" The minister put down his pen and sat back in his chair. Blushing deeply, Gillian remembered how as a teenager she had, like most of the other girls, wanted a white wedding in a church like this one. It hadn't occurred to her then that her not believing in God could be an obstacle, but it occurred to her now.

The minister folded his hands over his belly. "Gillian," he said. She was startled by his use of her first name. "Have you accepted Christ as your saviour?"

She looked down. "No," she whispered.

He leaned toward her. "Is your husband-to-be a Christian?" Gillian imagined the offence David would take at such a suggestion, and it brought a slight smile to her lips.

"No," she said again, "but his parents are." The minister cleared his throat. Gillian had another thought. "And the—the substitute—I mean the surrogate—who will stand in for my husband, he's a Christian." She pictured Harold, the Chinese boy a year younger than herself, whom she had asked to be David's surrogate, praying with eyes closed at the Christian youth group at her high school. But the good Reverend gazed at her, uncomprehending. She explained quickly.

"My husband—you see, we're already married—is in England. He...he can't come." She bit her tongue so as not to repeat the lie her mother was telling everyone, that David had broken his leg. "My parents want me to have a wedding ceremony here, because David and I eloped," she blushed deeply, "in England. The last time I was there. So my parents, they want me to have a Chinese wedding, and I—I thought—well,

I wondered about having it in your church."

Even now Gillian wasn't aware of how outlandish her request would sound to Reverend Dawes. He envisioned his church full of Chinese faces and incense, of a makeshift shrine to Buddha blocking the view of the altar, and for some reason, of chickens running wild in the aisles, squawking and flapping and leaving their droppings everywhere. He supposed that must be an image he'd seen, in some *National Geographic* magazine, of Chinese markets, where animals lived and were slaughtered amidst their own filth.

"Gillian," he said. He put his hands squarely on the desk and pushed himself into a standing position. He was tired. "I am afraid you will have to find somewhere else to hold your wedding." Gillian gazed up at him. He shook his bald head slightly, and it seemed to her quite pink, with the wreath of white wisps around it. Slightly sad, he looked at her kindly. "My child, this church is a house of God. I do not think my Bishop would… feel comfortable…with a Chinese wedding being held here."

Gillian looked down at her hands, and felt shame, as though a pure white light had been cast upon her heart and found it wanting. She held her purse in front of her lap, in her two hands and went out, into the sun and cold wind. She felt small and thin-shouldered, but her belly was heavy, weighing her down despite the cheerful gusts of air.

Gillian walked home, thinking of the way Reverend Dawes's bald spot had grown and spread like an advancing desert. She did not think about alternative venues for the wedding—the Legion, for example, or the old school house that was used as a community hall now. He had stood up, his hands on his desk, pink and rough as though he had been a working man all his life. His eyes were sad and kind, and made her feel somehow shrunken and despicable. She couldn't bear to remember those eyes, and put her sunglasses on.

Her mother was waiting for her when she arrived home. She had saved a bowl of noodles for her on the kitchen table, under a taut drum of Saran wrap, which always made Gillian think of something in a glass case in a museum. Knowing that Reverend Dawes would say no to a Chinese wedding in his church, Mrs. Wong had come up with a list of other possibilities, which included the Legion and the old school, but also some others—the hotel, which might be expensive; the high school auditorium; and the bowling alley.

"The bowling alley?" Gillian asked. She looked at the back of her mother's head, as she prepared a chicken for roasting. Mrs. Wong washed the nude carcass in the sink, as though she were bathing a newborn. Gillian put her hand on her belly. Mrs. Wong said, matter-of-factly, "Yes. Bowling alley has lots of room. Lots of places to sit, tables. Your…daddy…can walk with you along the aisle. The bowling alley."

"What?" Gillian asked, dumbfounded. "You mean you actually want me to get married in a lane at the bowling alley?" Her mother lifted the chicken out of the sink and set it to drain in the dish drainer, then turned around.

"Your choice," Mrs. Wong said firmly. Coldly. Gillian looked down. "I just give suggestions."

Gillian could see herself in the red and gold dress her mother was making for her (not a traditional Chinese wedding outfit but something like a mini dress sheath, though in traditional wedding colours). She pictured herself barefoot, sliding along the lane's shining hardwood in her stockings. All the guests had put on rented bowling shoes, and stood around in front of the pin-setting machines, where sets of pins stood ready to be knocked down. The lighting was dim except where the pins shone, in perfect position. Gillian smiled at the thought of Harold, the surrogate, slipping awkwardly around the lane in worn black and white bowling shoes. Then after the wedding, the guests drank and ate and bowled, and she danced with Harold, whose head bobbed like a male pigeon courting a female, but more out of apology for stepping on her feet than out of desire.

"Ma," Gillian said. "I think maybe the old school house."

Mrs. Wong wiped her hands on a tea towel. "It's pretty," she acknowledged. "So many trees. No kitchen though. But I make all the food at home."

That night Gillian dreamed of a wedding in the bowling alley. It was very dark, though the lights that lit up the pins gleamed off the floor of the lanes. When Harold tried to place the ring on her finger, he was so nervous he tripped in the gutter and plunged like a diver, his arms pointing out in front of him, and crashed into the pins.

"Strike!" a male voice called out from the dark. A crack opened and swallowed Harold, and then Gillian was in her bedroom, with Harold falling through the crack in her ceiling, but it wasn't Harold, it was David. Gillian lay in her bed, unable to move, as David fell toward her. Before he landed on top of her, she jerked awake and rolled to one side.

Nine

A nd so Gillian's Chinese wedding took place in the old
school house. There were still a couple old benches in
the back of the hall, to remind people of the building's past
purpose. There were initials carved into them, some with
hearts around them, some smooth-edged and traced by ball-
point pens, all of varying vintage. The floors were pine and
somewhat uneven, which gave it a funhouse kind of feel, Gillian thought. At the back of the school house, facing the front
door was a lectern, that, having been abandoned by the school
board, had been used by a wide variety of speakers throughout the years—political candidates, travelling preachers, high
school debaters, spelling bee contestants, and once, although
it was supposedly hush-hush, by a stripper who as part of her
stag party act pretended to be a randy schoolteacher.

Gillian had overheard this story at recess from some of the
boys in her class, who claimed to have crouched under the
windows the night of the stag party and watched the striptease,
which involved a pointer and a globe and a number of books.
They debated, in serious tones among themselves what exactly
had occurred, but they were clearly baffled.

Gillian noticed the grave and pensive absorption with which
they considered their homeroom teacher Mrs. Franklin, who
was a handsome woman of about forty with a knot of auburn
hair at the back of her neck. As though their night under the

window of the old school house had transformed for them a woman who might actually have been older than some of their mothers. The girls giggled when Mrs. Franklin rapped her desk with the pointer and the boys' mouths fell open and they blushed. Gillian blushed with them and sat at her desk looking straight ahead, as though nothing had happened. A thought about what would transpire if the story reached her parents' ears flitted through her mind, causing her a twinge of panic—how they would look at her differently, now that her own ears were sullied with dirt.

Thankfully, Mrs. Wong never did hear the story of what happened at the old school house. The caretaker, a retired handyman with a slight hunch that made him look like a bird, a heron or an egret, his baseball cap jutting out in front of him like a bill, let Gillian and her mother into the building. Gillian was almost afraid the stripper's ghost would be waiting to accost her mother—that there would be some hazy remnant of salacious energy floating around—but it was her mother who, in her usual prim and brisk way, took control of the place. Clutching her purse in front of her, she walked with small quick steps up the centre of the school house to where the lectern stood, faltering only slightly on the uneven floors. She sniffed the air, and ran a finger over the lectern.

"Dusty," she said and coughed slightly into her handkerchief.

Gillian couldn't tell if it was a fake cough. She said nothing, but wandered around the room, which smelled of old wood and chalk and cigarette smoke from the bingo games held there some weekends. She could imagine being married there, and pictured David leaning slightly to the left on the crooked floor as they stood in front of the lectern and said their vows to a justice of the peace. But it wouldn't be David, she remembered, and put her hand to her mouth.

Mrs. Wong peered out the window at the parking lot and

the dark weeds at its edge, poking out of the dirty snow. The windows were a little grimy, and the walls needed washing. She turned to the caretaker, who was fumbling with a sticky doorknob.

"Who will clean this place, if we have wedding here?" she asked, in a high sharp voice.

Gillian turned away, embarrassed. The caretaker took his hat off, wiped his gnarled hand across his brow, and looked squarely at Mrs. Wong.

"Missus, if you want it cleaned up better than it is now, you'll have to do it yourself," he said in a pleasant tone.

Mrs. Wong's eyes narrowed, then she nodded. "You take ten dollar off the price and we clean."

The caretaker nodded. "I'll have to ask my boss, but I'll see what I can do," he said, and, as they left the building, nodded congenially to Gillian's mother. She nodded back, clearly pleased.

Gillian, having barely left teenage-hood, still felt she was tagging along with her mother on one of their terrible shopping trips, when Mrs. Wong picked out all the wrong clothes for her and dismissed the jeans and flowing dresses Gillian chose with a wave of her hand. That is, until she started earning her own babysitting money and splurged on mini skirts and bell-bottoms, which her mother bore with indignant silence. Still, today Gillian felt humiliated and inconsequential as if the matter of her wedding were really nothing to do with her.

Which in a way, it wasn't. The whole matter of the Chinese wedding was to please her mother. Gillian sat down on one of the old school benches and put her head down, feeling her face grow hot. She wanted to stamp and shout, to feel the floor boards give way under her, but she realized then that it was a tantrum brewing, the sort in which a two-year-old indulged. In a wave of shame, she remembered that it had been her fault, after all, that she married David without any thought for her parents. Now she was determined she would endure all the suffering she had brought upon herself, without blaming her mother.

"Gillian," Mrs. Wong said, "you like?" Gillian took a deep breath and smiled and nodded. Mrs. Wong continued, gesturing to the windows. "We clean everything, like brand new," she said excitedly. "We put banners here, over the door—we have lots of flowers, peonies," she gestured to imaginary vases on either side of the lectern, "and food!" She spread out her arms. "Suckling pig. Roast duck, red bean pudding—must have red food for happiness! And for Chinese New Year."

Mrs. Wong put her hands out to cup her daughter's face, her jade bracelet slipping down to the little bone of her powdered wrist. It was the first time in a long time Gillian remembered her doing that. She was astounded to feel a surge of hot tears spilling out over her cheeks and her mother's hands. The unwept tears of anger and hurt that had inhabited her flesh for so many years, gushing out in a river of penance. The baby in her belly, released and floating like a balloon free from its tether.

Mrs. Wong smiled at her daughter and patted her wet cheeks tenderly. "You will be beautiful, a beautiful bride," she said gently. "Never mind David no here...he will understand."

When Gillian phoned David to tell him that it was all arranged, the Chinese wedding with a surrogate standing in his place, he was silent. Flabbergasted. Gillian, in a hushed monotone, told him about the old school house, the hours spent sponging the walls and wiping the windows, the preparations her mother was making for the banquet, the dress she would wear. David only asked, in a hoarse voice that made him sound as if he had a cold, who would his surrogate be? Gillian was quiet for a moment. It was only Harold, a boy she had scarcely looked at growing up. But she knew David would lie awake in bed, picturing him as aloof and handsome, a debonair Chinese. She smiled slightly, twisting the phone cord around her wrist.

"He's only a child, David."

He was not reassured. Gillian, he realized, was barely out of childhood herself. And he felt the distance between them, since he had brought her home to meet his parents. He had made a fatal mistake, he realized that. He had been both anxious and rebellious when he presented them with a wife with black hair and slanted eyes, a wife whom he loved but whom he did not consider at all, in that moment. Since then it seemed that the sail on the boat of their lives together had come loose and was flapping in the breeze.

"Gillian," David said. She didn't answer. "Gillian, I want to come there. I want to be with you." Still she said nothing. "I'll quit my job," he said in desperation. "I'll take what the pension fund owes me and fly out there tomorrow." There was silence on the other end of the phone.

Then Gillian said, faintly, "No, David." His heart crumpled. "It's all arranged. My mother has already ordered the flowers and banners and the roast ducks. She's in the kitchen right now, making dumplings."

David realized then that there was nothing he could do, if Mrs. Wong had her hands in the flour already. He felt his face sag, like that of a sad clown.

"Alright," he said, with difficulty. He told Gillian he loved her, that he thought about her every minute, that he would be there soon. Gillian was only half-listening. She watched her mother, arms covered in rice flour, forming the delicate morsels that she would drop in a pot of boiling water the morning of the wedding, a day from now. Gillian's stomach growled and she felt quite faint.

The phone slipped from her hand. Mrs. Wong, glancing up from her work, hurried to her side. Gillian's head felt damp but cool as her mother brushed a strand of hair from her face. She yelled for her husband and Gillian's eyes opened, staring up at her with the detachment of a stranger.

David heard the phone gently banging the leg of the chair, and a commotion on the end of the line. He listened intently for a moment, trying to understand what was going on.

"Gillian?" he asked. He heard Mr. Wong's "Ai-ya!"

"Gillian!" he yelled. Then Mrs. Wong's voice, hesitant and yet still clipped, came on the line.

"David. She no can talk. Feel sick. Call tomorrow." The receiver clicked as she put it down in the cradle.

David held the phone on his lap for a long time, as though it were a newborn baby, until the insistent beeping stopped and a smooth female operator's voice asked him to please hang up. The receiver's twisty umbilical cord wrapped around his wrist.

And he remembered something he had not thought of for many years. Swimming in a pond as a boy with a friend. They overturned a rubber dinghy, surfacing underneath it into the hollow of the hull. Singing a cheerful song with vulgar words their voices, loud and muffled at the same time, ricocheted off the walls of the hull. The water, lapping and sucking at the edges of the dinghy, dampened the echoes—it was as if they were in a cavernous grotto, far from England, far from anyone else they knew. His friend began to banter in the friendly, aggressive way of young boys. He shoved David's shoulder and splashed water in his face. David, bewildered, backed himself into the end of the dinghy, refusing to shout or shove back. The friend quickly tired of him, and saying that David was a bloody Irishman and had bad breath, he ducked underwater and out. My father was left, alone and aggrieved, like a man in the belly of a whale.

Ten

Gillian's parents ushered her to her room and she lay down on the bed. They loosened her blouse at the neck and covered her with her quilt. Gillian was able to speak by then and she tried to convince them she was fine, that she had merely fainted, that all she needed was a cup of tea. She gazed up at the crack in the ceiling above her bed while her mother hurried to the kitchen and her father sat on the edge of her bed and stroked her hand. He looked at her with kind eyes, his mouth agitated from trying not to cry. Gillian was too exhausted to do anything but close her eyes and squeeze his hand.

When she went to the doctor that afternoon, he told her she had anaemia, and prescribed iron pills. But her mother had other ideas.

"Humph," she snorted. "Your blood is tired. You must drink beef tea. I make for you." Gillian didn't put up a fight—she loved beef tea. She lay in her bed the day before her Chinese wedding, wishing that somehow, the world would just go away, and that she could sleep forever under her old quilt.

The beef tea simmered in a pot on the stove, wafting through the house as Mrs. Wong continued to make dumplings, their shapes like new daisy buds. Mr. Wong watched her from the doorway. Taking a long drag on his cigarette, he said in Chinese, "Gillian is not well enough to be married tomorrow." Mrs. Wong, not looking up, waved one floury hand at him.

"She is fine, just tired. Do you remember when I was pregnant with her, I fainted on board the ship to Vancouver?" Mr. Wong nodded. "All I needed was some strength in my blood. This soup is strength. She will be fine tomorrow."

And it seemed that she was right. Gillian sat up in bed and drank three bowls of beef tea, sucking on the tender meat and slurping the broth. The heat of it made her sweat but she felt the juices creeping through her. It was only her spirit that was still weak.

On the morning of her Chinese wedding, Gillian had beef tea for breakfast. Then she put on the lovely red and gold brocade sheath that her mother had made for her, and sat down in front of her dressing table. She looked at herself in the mirror, her face pale and solemn. At the front door, she heard her hairdresser Cindy, chewing a fresh stick of Wrigley's, with her unnatural blond curls piled up on her head, being greeted by her mother. She knew Mrs. Wong would give Cindy the ivory comb she had worn at her own wedding, and ask Cindy to make her daughter look like a beautiful Chinese doll.

Gillian knew she was too dispirited to put up a fight. She would let Cindy do as she liked, but she would not allow her face to be powdered white. Cindy rapped sharply on the door and let herself into the room with a couple tote bags full of her tools and product. Gillian smiled at her. Cindy's eyes widened.

"Gilly, you look soooo beautiful! What a sweet dress," she cooed. Gillian put her hand to her belly, and turned back to the mirror. Cindy, professional that she was, knew immediately that her customer wasn't in the talking mood. So she chattered away in her best hairdresser voice about things Gillian would have to neither care about nor feel the need to respond to, as she gazed down at her lap.

When the session was over, Gillian barely looked at herself. Cindy patted the towel across her shoulders.

"Gillian," she said softly, forcing her to look up. Cindy was about ten years older than Gillian, and apparent even under the caked on makeup, there were wrinkles starting around her mouth and the corner of her eyes. She had a truck-driving husband, a ten-year-old daughter and a boy in preschool. "Gillian you're breaking my heart," she said. "Look at yourself." She turned the bride's shoulders gently toward the mirror. Gillian shrugged, but looked. He hair was swept up on top of her head with a sprig of baby's breath and the ivory comb. Two twisty strands of hair framed her face—like the Hasidic Jews, those dark, skinny boys in skull caps she saw in Hyde Park, she thought and smiled glumly.

"There," Cindy squealed. "You should smile. You're some beautiful. That man of yours won't be able to resist you—" She stopped herself when she remembered that it was not "her man" Gillian was marrying, but a surrogate. "Oh damn. Sweetie, sorry. You just have fun. Your man would want you to be happy today." She took out her makeup. "Let me do your face. No extra charge," she added briskly.

When Gillian emerged from her bedroom—Cindy behind her, triumphant—her parents were waiting. Cindy made Gillian turn around so they could see how she had swept the bride's hair up off the back of her neck. Mrs. Wong gasped and put her hands to her mouth. And Mr. Wong, awe-struck, leaned against the wall and gaped. Gillian thought there was something wrong.

"Ma—what's the matter?" she asked. She wanted to go sit down at the kitchen table and drink tea. Her mother took her hand and squeezed it, afraid to hug her in case her makeup came off on her shoulder.

"So beautiful—my daughter," she said.

Eleven

David was flying from Britain, through the eternal blue of the upper atmosphere. The white blanket of cloud below him reminded him of the Arctic, a barren place, where the sun was bright enough to blind the hunters who travelled over the ice to hunt seal and polar bear. As the plane descended, into the grey mass of the cloud cover, tears of rain streamed across the airplane windows, and he could see nothing.

He caught a taxi to the Wongs' house, but they had already left for the school house. Frantic, he asked the taxi driver if he knew where to find the old school house that was now a rental hall. The cabbie grunted, his tobacco-stained fingers pointing up the road.

"It's about a mile up," he said. David asked him to take him there. "Chinese wedding up there today," he said. "I took an old chink couple up there earlier." David, stunned as if by a blow to the head, did not reply.

At the school house, he handed the cabbie a couple dollars and scrambled out of the car. He pulled his blazer on and ran up the steps to the double doors. Inside he could hear the muffled sound of the justice of the peace, clearing his throat. David opened the door to the sea of black-haired wedding guests, and the light from the grey sky fell just short of Gillian and Harold, standing at the front of the school house. Gillian, red and gold, turned and saw her husband, standing dishevelled in the doorway—it reminded her of how she had left him the first day they met in Hyde Park, as her bus pulled away from the curb and he stood with his arm in the air, as if hanging on to an invisible strap.

Although she had not envisaged him there, she felt no surprise, and no relief. She felt nothing. Someone snapped the photo just then, of her and Harold, looking back over their shoulders. They both turned back to the justice of the peace.

"I now pronounce you, David Simpson and Gillian Wong, man and wife."

This is how David interrupted his own wedding. And how Mrs. Wong, who had promulgated the fib about his having broken his leg, almost lost face with the entire Chinese community. But David, who saw the look of horror on her face as he stood in the doorway of the school house, remembered to limp, and spent the afternoon telling people that actually his leg had been badly sprained, that he was on the mend, that his mother-in-law had only slightly misunderstood him. Gillian stood beside him, saying little and smiling. David kept looking at her, encouraging and looking for encouragement but she merely smiled up at him, her dark eyes unreadable.

People began to push back the chairs and bring out the tables piled one on top of another at the back of the school house. They spread red paper tablecloths, and the women began to take out the food, from Tupperware containers and Saran-wrapped bowls. Mrs. Wong had been cooking for a week and Mr. Liu provided the duck and roast pork from his restaurant, for a good price. The lectern was moved and Gillian sat at the table at the front of the school house, with Harold on one side of her and David on the other side. David tried to make conversation with Harold but it was difficult with the noise of the other guests, shouting and toasting the married couple, feigning confusion about who the real husband was or making jokes to the Wongs about their daughter having two husbands.

Gillian, who barely spoke, felt the need to lie down. She clutched David's arm and tried to stand up but teetered as though her feet were bound. David held her in both arms, and there was a cry of alarm from Harold.

"David," Gillian said hoarsely. He bent his head, emotional and worried, to hear her. "Your leg." His chest deflated. He asked Harold to hold Gillian, since he could not carry her with his sprained leg, and stood back, as Harold, with difficulty, laid her down on the floor.

Which was, thankfully, clean from all the scrubbing Gillian and her mother had done. The bride looked up at the faces surrounding her. There was her mother, flushed red with guilt and worry; her father, pale as a rice dumpling; and her husband, his face dark with concern. All the people she loved. And then there was Harold, whose face bobbed over her, as though she were underwater and his head were a buoy on the surface.

Gillian closed her eyes and when she awoke she was back home in her bedroom. Her thoughts eddied and pooled, before being sucked away by some receding tide. It was over, she realized, amidst a swirl of memories of the taste of roast duck, the noise of the guests and the sight of her husband standing in the doorway of the school house, silhouetted by the light. The Chinese wedding. And she had failed.

Gillian felt the weight of that failure pressing her shoulders, her heart, her spine, down into the soft mattress. She knew that at some point in the future, a hook hanging in the water above her would pull her to the gleaming surface, but right now she would sleep. David's hand was brushing the hair from her forehead—she knew it was him by his scent—but someone cut the cord of the elevator and she was plummeting, without fear and without hope, to a dark and bottomless place.

Her husband's heart unhusked like a cob of corn. There she was, the woman for whom he had forsaken his job and country. She seemed small, barely making a bump under the old quilt, with a peaceful look under her smudged makeup. Her hair fanned out across the pillow, as though she were floating in a pool of water, like the Lady of Shallot.

Mrs. Wong opened the door quietly. "David," she commanded. "Come eat." Reluctantly, he rose from the edge of the bed and followed her to the kitchen, where Mr. Wong was reading the paper. He looked up at David and did not smile, but pulled out a chair for him.

Mrs. Wong set a bowl of noodle soup in front of him. Leftovers from the wedding, brought back to the house by guests in the back of their station wagons, sat uneaten on the counter. The guests had also taken mounds of food home, but there was still enough left to feed Mao's army.

"David," Mrs. Wong began. "Gillian is pregnant." David looked stunned. She nodded, and for clarification added, "Your baby. She no tell you because she think you quit your job and come to Canada too soon," she continued. "But that no matter now. You here."

Despite his exhaustion and worry, David felt a small seed of joy lodge itself in his heart. He put a hand to his throat, which suddenly seemed too dry to talk.

"Gillian's blood is tired," Mrs. Wong said. "She need lots of rest. Getting married is too much for her. We should have waited," she admitted, her bottom lip trembling.

David felt a wave of tenderness for these parents of his bride. He held Mrs. Wong's hand awkwardly, as she brushed tears from her eyes. Mr. Wong put his paper down, and though his face was like a stone, his eyes glistened. David wanted to comfort them, in the only way he knew how. He began to eat, slurping the noodles from his bowl as he had seen an old man do in a Chinese restaurant in London. Mrs. Wong got up and brought him a bowl of dumplings and roast duck and pork, which left their bright red stain on his fingers and teeth. Grateful and contrite, she smiled at him through her tears.

Twelve

G illian stayed in bed for a week, with David sleeping on a cot beside her. She sat up to take her iron pills, to drink beef tea and nibble at wedding leftovers, but it seemed the act of eating left her more tired than before. She would lie down, and David, lying on the cot, would hold her hand and tell her stories, about pirates who had a parrot that spoke Japanese and gave them away as they tried to overrun a Chinese navy ship in the dead of night; about a girl who grew antlers and ran off to join a herd of reindeer, and a rabbi who attracted butterflies, which covered him in a shimmering coat of many colours. David, who had never before told a story in his life, would get lost in his rambling plots while Gillian clung weakly to the thread that would lead her out of the labyrinth of these haphazard tales. Her eyes would begin to close and, still clinging to the life-line David had thrown her, she would descend into the well of sleep, searching for something she could never find, in the sinking darkness.

The Saturday a week after the Chinese wedding, while David was still asleep, Gillian got out of bed and, one hand on her sunken belly, made her way to the kitchen. She poured some tea from the thermos on the kitchen table and sat down carefully in her usual place. The sun was just beginning to creep over the horizon, and the starlings, black and huddled in the branches of the tree in the backyard, were beginning to rustle and chirp. My mother took her iron pill and watched the steam rising silently from her tea, delicate as a pea vine climbing into the empty air. It made her think of her father's cigarettes, which for the most part she hated, except for the way the smoke unfurled from their ends, dreamlike and meditative.

Mrs. Wong, eyes half-closed, entered the kitchen in her bathrobe.

"Hi Ma," Gillian said, in a voice that was slightly hoarse from disuse.

Mrs. Wong startled. "Gillian, you get up?" she asked, as if she could not quite believe it. Her daughter nodded. "You feel stronger?" She nodded again. "You want eat? Beef tea from yesterday still good."

Gillian shook her head. "No more beef tea, Ma."

Mrs. Wong sat down across the table and my mother poured her a cup of tea from the thermos.

"Gillian." Her hands were trembling. "I sorry. No good to have wedding when your blood is so tired. I make mistake. Sorry." Mrs. Wong's cheeks, her daughter noticed, were not as round and full as they should be—drawn, she thought, from worry.

"Don't, Ma," she whispered, and with some effort she searched her mind for a comforting thing to say. "David is here now, and I am glad. The wedding brought him here."

As if on cue, David, dishevelled and groggy, came into the kitchen, and as though he were just passing through the door between sleep and wakefulness, his eyes brightened and his face shifted. Smiling eagerly, he sat down beside her, and two things struck her. One, that there was a light in his face that made her seem dark by comparison. And that although the beef tea and rest had given her back her physical strength, she was weakened by love. She was under no illusion that David was any stronger, just that he had not yet succumbed to disappointment, along the path of his love for her, the way she had along the path of her love for him.

When Mr. Wong came into the kitchen, bare-chested in his pyjama pants, he stopped short at the sight of my mother, gazing up at him. He held up both arms as though he had just scored a soccer goal, and the Chinese newspaper he held, curled into a telescope, touched the ceiling.

Thirteen

David managed to get a job at the hospital—it wasn't as senior a position as he'd held in England but it was a start, and because of it, he and Gillian, with help from her parents, were able to buy a bungalow a few miles away from them and next door to the Jamiesons' and the Tulleys'. The Wongs would have liked them to be closer, but Gillian knew that in order to be free from the tether that bound her to her past, she needed distance between them—even though the future yawned before her like a dark cavern.

I was born the day after my parents had their first fight—or rather, after the first time my mother snapped at my father. Gillian was lying in bed, exhausted, her belly as round as a watermelon. She felt my feet, jerking rather gently and rhythmically, against her ribs, and it occurred to her that her child was bored and fidgeting, that the wait to be born was as hard on the baby as it was on her. It was Friday night and David was watching the news on television. She called to him to bring her a glass of iced tea, which he did, in a blue ceramic cup that he'd bought at a summer craft sale, and flopped down beside her on their bed. David, still lanky as a teenager, was growing a beard which he intended to shave when the baby was born.

"Like hockey players in the Stanley Cup finals," he proudly told his co-workers, but really he had no interest in sports—it was a Che Guevara look that he was after.

He rubbed his beard against his wife's belly. She fished an ice cube out of the cup of iced tea and began to draw on the taut balloon below her ribs.

"David, do you think the baby can feel this?" she asked. As if in response, I kicked hard inside her, and she gasped. Her husband put his hand on her rippling belly and declared, "This one's going to be a football player."

"Either that or a juvenile delinquent," Gillian countered glumly, "kicking his own mother like that."

David wondered what effect the suction from a bathroom plunger would have on his unborn child, but Gillian, overcome with fatigue, told him she didn't think it was a good idea. David rubbed her back, and she made her way into a dreamless thicket of sleep. What about suction, my father continued to wonder. Would the baby respond to slight suction, something less drastic than a plunger? He tried to imagine what he could use. The cup might work. The Chinese used cupping to treat a number of ailments, he had heard from a Chinese doctor at the hospital in London. It seemed to him Dr. Li had told him that the cups were heated to produce suction.

David took the cup that contained the last of the iced tea and drank it down, pouring the remnants of ice cubes out into a potted plant. Now, how did Dr. Li say it was done, he wondered. Ah, yes. He found a chopstick in the kitchen drawer and some rubbing alcohol and cotton balls in the bathroom. Sitting on the toilet seat, he soaked a cotton ball in alcohol, pressed it down onto the end of the chopstick and lit it with a match. It flamed like a marshmallow at a campfire. He inserted the burning end into the cup and felt the sides warm up. Then he left everything except the cup in the bathroom sink and returned to the bedroom.

David placed the open end of the cup on my mother's side, below her ribs. As the ceramic cooled, the suction created tugged her skin up into the ring of the cup's edge. David put his hand on her belly to see if the baby was stirring, but I was asleep inside my mother, unmoved by the cup which sucked at her womb the way the moon's gravitational field tugs at the ocean.

David sighed—his child had failed to respond to his experiment. It was the first time he felt disappointment in relation to me, the flesh of his flesh, before he and I had even been officially introduced.

The lifespan of David's curiosity was limited. He tugged gently at the cup stuck to his wife's stomach, but it was not enough to pull it loose. He realized, with a sinking feeling, that it was going to take a sustained effort for it to come off. Taking the cup in both hands, he pulled hard and it released with a loud sucking sound. Gillian, startled, awoke. There was fear and confusion in her eyes.

"David, what are you doing?" She looked down at herself and saw the red ring, and tried to brush it away with her hand, as though it were a fly that had landed on her.

David quaked with shame. "I...I was trying some cupping on you, to see whether the baby would respond."

Gillian's eyes darkened. "Cupping?"

He stammered, "Yes, yes, cupping... it's an ancient...it's a Chinese medicine practice. I thought maybe...the baby might move...from the suction..." He pleaded with his eyes for mercy. But she was furious. He had never seen her this way before. Her face was dark as a thundercloud, her eyes spitting lightning.

"David, I'm so tired I can barely see," was all she said, but her voice was laden with dire significance. He looked down and tugged anxiously at his beard. Gillian rolled on to her side, away from him.

And that was all—but it was the first time his wife had

expressed displeasure with him and, he lay beside her, shattered. She was already asleep again but her breathing sounded exasperated. For the first time it occurred to him that it was strange that they had never fought, that she had never said an unkind word to him. That such an unnatural situation could not possibly last. Even after the fiasco of her first meeting with her parents, she hadn't said an angry word or expressed her hurt. He realized now that he had not opened the door for her, that perhaps there were many things she wanted to say, but hadn't. David, who had always believed in the possibility of utopia, felt cast out. He had been living in paradise, but now the door to Eden was shut and he was standing on the outside, naked and alone.

Fourteen

Before Gillian awoke the next morning, David crept out of bed and made her a pot of coffee. He felt timid in the face of her anger the night before, and decided to go to the hospital to finish off some paperwork, to fortify himself. Then he would take her out for supper, apologize for his reluctance—his inability—to encourage an open discussion of his failings and her feelings. And if the chance arose, he would begin a conversation specifically about the moment he introduced her to his parents. The idea made him sweat, but he realized he felt as though he were walking across the sea on inflated inner tubes, and that he needed the solid ground beneath him once more.

But my mother and father never did have that conversation, because early in the afternoon, I was born.

Gillian was awakened by a contraction, but had read enough to realize that labour in earnest could be many hours away. She waddled out to the kitchen, sat down with a magazine and poured a cup of coffee. She had almost forgotten about the cupping incident the night before, but realized, in her sleepy state, that somehow, something had been broken.

Gillian considered this event in a dispassionate, almost absent-minded way. She sat at the table, stirring milk and sugar into her coffee, until she realized that she did not drink it that way. It was her husband who took milk and sugar.

Her mind kept flitting back to this mistake as she spent

the morning washing the breakfast dishes, vacuuming and washing the kitchen floor. Gillian had never liked housekeeping, but it seemed that expecting a baby had triggered some need for cleanliness in her. It also helped keep her mind off the contractions.

In the sliding glass door to the back yard, she caught sight of her reflection—holding one hand under her belly while pushing the Hoover with the other. She was astounded to see a pregnant housewife with a tired, pale face and a mess of hair tied up in an old scarf. Since the Chinese wedding she had had trouble looking at herself in the mirror, and now she was seized with an anxiety that she had never felt before—the need to become someone, quickly, before it was too late.

She sat on a dining room chair. Her face gleamed up at her from its dark surface. Between contractions, which seemed to her just a bit stronger and more frequent, she realized she had never really thought she needed a career—it just hadn't occurred to her. Nothing really aroused her passion, or indeed, even interested her very much, except finding a husband to live with, happily ever after. She had never thought of this goal as anything but normal, never felt limited or oppressed by it. And now that her child was about to be expelled from her womb, the lifelong career of motherhood, to which she had given so little thought, loomed before her like a prison sentence.

Gillian had been a decent and dutiful student, but mostly she had spent her time in school being miserable, and worrying about whether the other girls liked her. Trying to be invisible and yet part of the crowd—trying, in fact, to be white. But she had come to terms with that, she thought evenly, clutching her belly. David's failure to inform his parents that she was Chinese had overshadowed all the insults of her past, and even that, she thought, she had come to terms with.

It occurred to her, as she shined her face in the dining room table with her shimmy cloth, that she had always liked arithmetic, adding up columns of numbers, subtracting, multiplying, dividing. Working on the neat rows of problems in dark pencil in her scribbler, she could forget for awhile the intensity of her self-consciousness, the chaotic jabber of her classmates, the memory of being called "chink" at recess by a girl who had been her friend the day before.

But it wasn't so much that she enjoyed math as that it made her forget herself. Her breathing relaxed and she was content, making her way through the rows and columns, like a gardener tending an orderly vegetable patch. Perhaps this is what happiness is—to be engaged in an activity that allows us to forget ourselves. It is not an emotion, an attitude, or a set of circumstances. It is that state of being unselfconscious, like Adam and Eve in the Garden of Eden before they took that fateful bite of fruit.

Gillian got up from the dining room chair. It was raining, so she went to find her rain poncho, one of the few things that fit her these days. She put on her husband's rubber boots, and went out into the back garden to pick the last of the season's tomatoes. The rain, which hissed as it fell into the long grass beyond the tomato patch, had already made puddles along the path between the rows of plants. The mud sucked at her boots, as though trying to hold her back. She plucked a tomato, not perfectly red, from a vine whose top was already withering, and placed it in the metal colander she had brought for that purpose. She would have to pick them all, she thought, since frost was in the forecast. So she picked another and another, then was almost knocked flat by a contraction, just before her water broke. It was my doing. Bored and impatient to be born, I pressed the elevator button, and made Gillian Simpson a mother.

Fifteen

I stare out the window of my parents' kitchen. My father is in the yard, sitting on a garden chair and reading the paper. It is one of those hazy golden days in September, the kind that makes you think the world is ending, and all the beauty in it has been distilled into one afternoon.

My father smokes a pipe since he retired, but only outside—my mother won't allow it in the house, not even in his study, though she tolerates his cigars on special occasions. The pipe, my father says, helps him think. I watch the bluish smoke rising as he puffs, his back to me. I know that in about ten minutes he will wander into the house, ostensibly for another cup of coffee but really to make sure I'm on my way to pick up the primary students.

The five-year-olds, with their silky hair and brand new skin, are runny-nosed and cheerful, except when they are runny-nosed and crying. They're almost too perishable—like rose buds from South America—to be transported in a rickety old bus with maroon vinyl seats by someone of my undepend-ability. It makes me miserable to realize this, so I try to ignore them, just drive the bus, just get to the next stop and make it in time to pick up the older kids at three-thirty. It's hard to keep my eyes open since I was up at five-thirty to take the kids to school for eight-thirty a.m. I drink coffee all day long but it doesn't seem to help. Once already, I've been late by about five minutes when I should have been five minutes early to pick up the primaries, because I had to make a detour to buy some cough drops to soothe my anxiety. Driving a bus full of kids is not a peaceful job, and when my nerves jangle I need a Halls. Last time, in line at the drugstore I was so distressed at being late for work that I couldn't stand still, and the people in line in front of me parted like the Red Sea for Moses, and let me through to the cash.

My boss told me she was not impressed, and that I had better not be late again or she would have to consider letting me go. But before she can fire me, I'm quitting—this afternoon—because even though it's only a week into the back-to-school season, I know I can't carry on. When I'm driving, especially the primaries, I feel like some strange marsupial with all her kittens holding on to her underbelly for dear life, and I can't bear the thought of some terrible accident that will make them lose their grip and fall to the forest floor.

I am almost thirty now, and I am still bored and drifting, and sometimes seized with a nameless anxiety. Whereas once the future was something to be met with eager anticipation, now I feel a constant, low-grade fear, and boredom has become a kind of refuge. It's as though the time to be born has passed and I am stuck floating in the womb, with the desire to propel myself forward suspended—as though the power went out in a tall building and the elevator is hanging inside a dark shaft by its cord, like some overripe fruit.

My father scrapes his feet on the outdoor mat and knocks his pipe against the door frame. "Joan," he says, stepping into the kitchen. I look up at the clock, and sure enough, it's time to leave.

"Thanks Dad, I'm going," I say, grabbing my coat from the hook by the door. He stares after me, half critically and half concerned, I think. It makes my heart shrivel with humiliation.

I drive my dad's car to the school bus depot, about ten minutes from where we live. All the yellow school buses are lined up in the parking lot, and a couple of the drivers, men in their fifties or sixties are standing around smoking. They wave politely, but I know they wonder what's wrong with me, a young woman with a couple university courses under her belt, driving a school bus—they think of me as some kind of loser, I imagine, even though they're doing the same job. At least they have families to support and no higher education.

It was my mother who told me about the job. She keeps her eye on the municipal government employment postings, and since she knows I like to drive, she thought this was something I might enjoy and stick with. Even though I was enthusiastic at first, especially when I passed my class two driver's licence test, the feeling petered out over the first couple days of work.

I was so nervous the first day when the kids piled in that I downed three Halls in fifteen minutes, sucking at them till my cheeks ached, and my tongue went numb. I drove that bus until it was time to quit and I told my supervisor, Jane, that I didn't think I could continue. She looked at me, over her bifocals and from under her pert salt and pepper hairdo and said, "Don't you think you just have the first day jitters? You did so well during training." I didn't know whether to be relieved or panic. Could it be first day jitters, after all? No, no I knew I was going to have a nervous breakdown if I had to do this job one more day. But all I said was I'd give it a try the next day and see.

When I got home that evening, my parents seemed to know not to ask me about how the day went. My father retired as usual to his study and my mother and I sat in the semi dark of the living room, me watching TV and her reading a cookbook. I felt her eyes on me, but she said nothing.

The next day, I was determined to stay calm. The kids were pretty well-behaved and didn't cause me any grief. The cough drops helped. And over the weekend, as I lay on a towel in the backyard to catch the last rays of summer, blissfully content, my parents quietly fidgeted in their lawn chairs, commenting on the poor state of the grass and finally, to my relief, asking me how I liked the job. Calmly, I said I liked it fine. My father looked slightly perturbed, and my mother gazed at me for a brief second, but then clapped her hands and said we should order in fried chicken to celebrate.

But on Monday, while I was taking the primary kids home, one of them peed his pants and the little girl next to him, ooing with disgust, hopped out of her seat while the bus was moving and fell in the aisle. She began to cry and another little girl started up too, out of sympathy, and the little boy who'd peed his pants leaned over his knees and sobbed. I stopped the bus and tried to calm them down but it made the kids more upset to see me walking down the aisle toward them. Though I spoke quietly and gently at first it was to no avail—they bleated piteously, like lost sheep. My forehead was sweating and my hair felt limp and stringy. I made a jerking motion with my arms, as though I were throwing something on the floor.

"That's enough!" I shrieked.

I had to drive, so I did, gritting my teeth all the way. When I got to my first stop, a couple mothers were there to meet their children and I grinned a terrible grin and told them a few of the kids were upset, but by now it was pretty much the whole bunch of them, and there was a smell of urine wafting up from the middle of the bus.

The mothers looked horrified. Their kids scrambled off the bus, weeping, and the women looked at me accusingly. What could I do? I shut the door and continued to my next stop.

When I got back to the depot that afternoon, Jane looked over her glasses at me and told me the mothers had called with concerns about my ability to comfort and control the kids. I agreed with them wholeheartedly—I wasn't equipped for this job. When things were calm, it had been fine but how long could I expect that to last, transporting a busload of five-year-olds? Then I thought of my father and how he despaired of my ever finding work that I could stick to. I couldn't quit. I couldn't bear to see his face. But I had to quit. For the first time I wanted to talk to my therapist.

Sixteen

I was almost five years old, sitting on the front steps of our house, a little bungalow with a pear tree flowering in the front yard. My mother sat beside me in her apron, peeling potatoes and dropping them into a big pot of water. She was talking to Edna, our neighbour Dr. Jamieson's housekeeper, whose last name I couldn't pronounce.

"You call me Edna," she said in a strong Hungarian accent, proudly crossing her arms across her ample bosom. "Edna is my Canadian name."

I was a little afraid of Edna. She was big and loud, and didn't mince words. I was eating an ice cream cone, Neapolitan, slowly turning it in my little hands and licking each side equally. It was serious work, and I didn't want to be deterred. I turned my back slightly so Edna couldn't see.

There was a bird singing in the pear tree, lost somewhere among the blossoms. I imagined the pear tree as a beautiful cage and the bird as a captive, trying to sing its way out. If only it found the right notes, a door would magically open and the bird would be free. But it sang the same lovely plaintive notes over and over again—then, when it did not receive an answer, it flew off.

Edna watched the bird fly from the pear tree. "That bird is looking for his wife," she said, in a tone that would bear no contradiction. I peered up at her. How did Edna know that? As if she heard my thoughts, she looked down at me, and in her eyes were both ferocity and kindness. "All birds look for their wife in spring. It is the time for weddings."

The idea that animals had weddings was one I knew from the poem "The Owl and the Pussycat," which my mother and father had both read to me. I imagined the bird in a little top hat and tails, his wing around another bird that looked exactly the same, except she had a white veil with tiny flowers on her head. They were in the heart of the pear tree, surrounded by white blossoms. In my imaginings, there was no minister, and no guests—only a picture of Chairman Mao. The birds simply bowed three times to the Dear Leader, as my father explained was the way the Chinese married, and flew off to make their nest.

There was a muddy "O" around my mouth, and ice cream dripping from my hands. My mother took no notice. She wasn't fastidious in the way some mothers are. She would just wipe my hands and let me play in my dirty clothes until bedtime, when she would throw them to soak in a tub of water. Or if we were going out, she would help me change into a fresh outfit, but would make me put my soiled clothes back on again to play in the garden.

Edna bent down quickly and grabbed my hand. "Look at what a mess you are," she clucked. Caught off-guard, I let my ice cream cone drop from my hand. I watched it roll around the pivot of its pointed end, as though it were inscribing a circle on the paved walk. Edna was immediately contrite.

"I'm sorry, honey," she said. My mother, as though noticing me for the first time, looked bewildered and slightly taken aback by Edna's lunging across her toward me. But she quickly regained her composure—Gillian was proud that she could meet Edna head-on, where other women in the neighbourhood would do anything to avoid her.

"You come to Dr. Jamieson's house. I give you poppy seed cake," Edna said. I looked up at my mother, who nodded and winked.

"Just as long as you bring back the recipe," she said, straight-faced. Edna laughed, her voice as big as a house.

"I no give you recipe unless you teach me good English," Edna countered. My mother thought for a moment.

"Okay, Edna, it's a deal," my mother said, "you give me your recipes and I will teach you English."

"I only make joke." Edna blushed, "My English is good. I give you recipe if this one likes poppy seed cake."

I had never been to Dr. Jamieson's house without my mother. Sometimes she and Edna would chat in Dr. Jamieson's kitchen, while Edna was washing dishes or preparing lunch. My mother would smoke a cigarette, something she never did at home, and sometimes she would take a sip from a bottle of clear liquid that Edna kept under the kitchen sink. My mother would never let me try it, but Edna let me smell it. Mixed in with the cool burning scent of alcohol was the sharp odour of pine needles. It reminded me of a Christmas tree. I wondered if this watery looking drink was made from the old Christmas trees.

"That's right," my mother said, smiling slightly and bending her head toward me. "Don't tell your father. He'll be upset." I nodded solemnly. He would certainly be upset, because he had told me that old Christmas trees go back to the North Pole to wait for next year. He didn't know they were made into a drink that Edna kept under the kitchen sink.

There was a muteness about the Jamiesons' house—a kind of muffled stillness that made my ears feel like they were stuffed up with cotton. Maybe it was the shag carpets that dampened sound or the dimness of the light that came through the white synthetic sheers, but it felt as though I was in a box shut up in someone's attic. I could never spend very long there without feeling like I was being suffocated.

Edna patted a seat at the kitchen table to indicate I should sit down. This was Edna's territory, and I knew to obey her every whim, or disaster might strike. I sat meekly, looking up at the collection of china plates that Mrs. Jamieson, who had no children and worked as a librarian, kept above the window over the kitchen sink. Edna hummed a melody I had heard her sing before, her voice strangely sweet and plaintive, as if she had forgotten she was in some Canadian kitchen. I surveyed her vast hips, her plump arms billowing as she cut the cake.

Edna's size and loudness seemed out of place in this small, orderly kitchen. Edna did not exactly belong, but I felt something like a candle in my chest for the woman. The candle wavered when Edna scolded me, but disapproval was always followed by a hug that drew me into her soft bosom. She also liked to feed me strange and wonderful things, like soups with meatballs, fried cheese, and now poppy seed cake.

I knew what poppies were. They were the huge red flowers in my mother's garden, whose petals scattered luxuriantly in a rainstorm. They looked almost animal, those blooms, with their hairy fronds and bulbous heads. But I had never seen the seeds, and the thought of eating them troubled me slightly, as though they might take root in my stomach. I knew sunflower seeds came from the heads of sunflowers, and as they slowly turned to follow the sun, birds would hang on to the heads with their little claws and eat the seeds before my mother had a chance to cut them down. The idea disturbed me, as though the birds were pecking away at the eyes and face of a sentient creature, one that I had watched grow from a tiny seedling to a towering giant.

Edna poured me a glass of milk and brought a slice of poppy seed cake to the table. I looked at it uncertainly. It was white on top and bottom with a dull, grey-black layer in between. Edna beamed and nodded toward the plate.

"Eat," she said. "Go on. You like." I had no choice. I took the fork and carefully cut a bite-sized piece. Little black poppy seeds rolled onto the plate. Edna smiled and nodded.

The texture was strange—a little bit sandy, but also smooth. The poppy seeds had been ground into a paste with sugar, and tasted sweet. I had never eaten food this colour before. I took a gulp of milk. Edna patted my cheeks fondly with both her hands.

"Poppy seeds very special. Expensive," she said. "It needs many poppies to make just one cake. You like?" she demanded. I nodded, and Edna chucked me under the chin, looking pleased. "Dr. Jamieson like too. I make this one for his birthday." She leaned toward me conspiratorially. "Mrs. Jamieson, she say she like it. But she never ask me for recipe."

I looked up into Edna's face, so close to my own. Edna had a small bump on her chin with a couple hairs growing from it. Her gold cross, hanging on a chain about her neck, swung toward me and back, like a pendulum. The little figure of Christ, head bowed and wearing a crown of thorns, hit me in the cheek as Edna kissed the top of my head. It felt sharp and cool.

While I ate, Edna worked on writing out the recipe for poppy seed cake. She had to translate it in her head and then transcribe the words in her fine scrawl. It took her a long time, during which she muttered to herself and droplets of sweat appeared on her brow. I felt as though the ceilings and walls were slowly, slowly closing in on us and the butterfly of my heart struggled to be released from my chest cavity. Finally though, Edna sighed and wiped her face with a tea towel. She smiled at me and took my hand, and led me out of that place.

My mother was hanging clothes on the washing line when Edna dropped me off. Edna triumphantly produced the index card on which she had written the recipe. I could tell my mother had forgotten all about it, but she pretended as though she had been waiting for it, and put it for safekeeping in her apron pocket.

Edna bent down to kiss my hair. "Soon you go to school," she said. "You no forget me. Come see me." Her mouth was puckered as though from a lemon and I thought she would cry. My mother touched Edna's hand. School was surely a terrible place, if Edna feared it would make me forget her.

I played in the yard all afternoon. It was flat and grassy, with a hedge between our backyard and the Jamiesons' on one side, and the Tulleys' on the other. I liked to lie in the grass, chin in my hands, watching small ants making their way along blades of grass. I liked to dig for worms and make little castles of fresh earth for them; make soup for my mother and me out of water and dirt and dandelion petals. To wash my hands under the outdoor faucet and drink from the stream of water before it fell to the ground. And to bury my face in a fresh sheet hanging on the line, if I wasn't too dirty. There were other children on our street but I didn't play with them. My mother wasn't interested in meeting other women her age; except for her visits with Edna she mostly kept to herself when she was home with me, and spent her time doing chores around the house and studying bookkeeping by correspondence.

Sometimes Edna would wave to me from next door when she put out the kitchen trash, and occasionally Dr. Jamieson would be out there with his clippers, puffing on his pipe, and raise a hand in greeting to me. I never saw Mrs. Jamieson, and the Tulleys were very old people who seemed to stay inside all the time, except for their weekly trips to the grocery store and to church, when they'd totter out together to their old sedan. But I was happy to be alone in my world, and even when my mother took me to the playground down the street, I kept to myself while the other children shouted and giggled and bickered. My mother sat on a bench, in a headscarf and dark sunglasses, and read a paperback while I rocked back and forth on a dolphin-like creature that was attached to the earth by a heavy spring. I imagined flying over the ocean on its back, my feet just skimming the tops of the waves.

That night while my mother was brushing my teeth, she muttered over the poppy seeds stuck between them, and the way the toothpaste foamed grey. She took me back downstairs to say goodnight to my father, and while he read me a story, my mother pulled Edna's recipe from her pocket. She squinted in the lamplight and frowned trying to make out Edna's hand-writing. I thought the spidery blue scrawl looked half magical. Of course I couldn't read it, but I was amazed that Edna's big hands, muscular from kneading bread and rough from scrub-bing floors and vegetables could produce something so fine. I thought about Edna's vastness, her warmth, her body puffing out like rising bread dough. Edna was what I knew her to be, but something else as well, something almost opposite. Not like in fairy tales, where the witches were ugly and evil and the princesses, good and delicate and beautiful, always. My father's story droned on. My mother put the recipe card in her pocket, and I watched a small spider slowly creep along the edge of the lampshade. I decided I would go to school to learn to write like Edna.

Seventeen

When I get home from driving the school bus on the afternoon of the weeping five-year-olds, I shut myself in my bedroom and call my shrink to leave a message on his machine. Forty-five minutes later, he calls back. He sounds pleased that I have called him, probably because during our sessions I am usually as "avoidant" as possible, not making eye-contact, not even raising my voice to a conversational level. His voice is sunny and eager as usual, but also concerned. I blurt out that I have to quit my job. He is silent for a few seconds, pondering, and then he asks, "Why?" He sounds genuinely interested.

But his curiosity is an affront. I feel anger rising up in me and clutching at my throat.

"Why?" I counter. "Because I can't stand the stress."

My shrink is quiet again. Then he asks, in what he must think is a gently probing but conversational tone, "What's causing your stress?"

"My job," I say out loud through gritted teeth.

"Yes, but what specifically about your job is causing you stress?" he asks pleasantly. "For example, are you having difficulty getting along with your co-workers? Your supervisor? Do the tasks of the job require skills or talents that you don't have or need to learn? You're good at math I know so I would have thought you amply qualified to work as a cashier." I realize then that my therapist doesn't know I'm driving a bus full of kids. Have I not told him? It has been almost a couple months since our last visit, since he'd been at an ashram in India for the summer, and obviously he still thinks I'm working at the grocery store where my mother was a bookkeeper. But that hadn't worked out because I couldn't concentrate—I always felt my mother's hopeful eyes on me, boring down into the back of my skull from her upstairs office.

As calmly as possible I tell him, "I'm working as a school bus driver now."

There is silence on the end of the phone. I picture him sitting in his plush chair at his desk and leaning forward slightly, toward me.

"I can't stand it," I say and start to cry. "I am so afraid something terrible will happen. My parents want me to keep this job but I just...can't," I say.

My shrink then says the one thing I had hoped for from him.

"Joan. Quitting this job doesn't mean you're a failure." I hold my breath. "It means you have enough concern for your own well-being and that of the children that you recognize you can't do this job, and you are willing to give it up. That takes strength of character," he continues. "I think recognizing your own limitations is a sign of your maturity."

I am so relieved I sob.

"There, there," he soothes. I reach for the Kleenex box. "You know yourself pretty well, Joan," he says, "but we all learn more about ourselves from experiences like this, when we venture out a little beyond our depths." He almost sounds wise. But he continues. "The universe allows us to take risks, to make mistakes, and even to fail to express the goodness inherent in all human beings—but it also catches us when we fall. We're here to learn," he asserts, passionately, almost...patriotically. "We're all students here, and Life is the great teacher. Have you read Lao Tzu?" he burbles on enthusiastically. "He says something like this. Good fortune leans against bad fortune… and within good fortune, bad fortune is hidden. That means that our good fortune and bad fortune need one another, indeed you might say, one is the seed of the other…" He's musing now. I'm not listening. I'm exhausted and scratching around in my pocket for a cough drop.

"Thanks Dr. Bard," I say, interrupting his monologue. He stops talking, and I can feel his woundedness on the other end of the phone, but also his gentle kindness. I relent. "I…I'm sorry," I say, "but I'm not in the mood for philosophy right now. I feel too…stuffed up and very tired. I appreciate your help, though."

"That's fine Joan," he says. "I'm glad to have helped. I guess you have an appointment coming up soon, so maybe we'll talk more then?"

I nod, and remember to say, "yes, see you then," before I hang up. The cough drop soothes me, and the numbness of my mouth makes me sleepy. I only half hear my mother gently knocking on the door to wake me for supper, and instead of getting up, I doze through the whole evening and on into the night.

I wake in the morning with a fuzzy head from too much sleep, determined that this afternoon I will quit my job. I feel peaceful, even serene, and in control. It is quitting a job, I realize now, that seems to bring out the best in me. I'll drive the bus today, if I must, but that's it—I won't give them two weeks notice or I'll be a babbling wreck by the end of it.

At the bus depot, I go straight up to Jane's office. A squiggle of anxiety worms its way through my stomach so I know I had better get it over with. I am determined to go cough-drop free this time. She looks at me over her bifocals and folded her hands on top of the papers on her desk. I don't bother with a preamble.

"I have to quit," I say.

She looks at me for some time, without saying anything. The golden chain attached to the arms of her glasses sways slightly. Then she says, "I know."

The worm of anxiety twists into a knot.

"What?" I ask, confused.

She repeats, slowly, as if I am a child, "I know...I know you have to quit."

My foot begins to twitch.

"It's alright. Not everyone is cut out for this job. Sometimes it's just the first day people have trouble, but some people have a lot of anxiety about driving a bus-load of kids, and that doesn't always go away."

It's true—she's right. But is it really so obvious that I am one of the unchosen?

"Your mother called," she says.

I look at her, uncomprehending.

"She has been worried about you," my supervisor continues. "She said you were crying last night and that you'd been unusually...well, that you hadn't been quite yourself."

It's a little bit too much to take in. My mother? Doesn't she trust me to handle this situation on my own? I stare blankly at my hands lying limp in my lap. They are slightly damp from sweat and it occurs to me they look strange and unfamiliar—almost as though I have never seen them before and don't know what they are.

"Joan," Jane begins, tipping her head to one side. I look up at her. "I'm glad you came to me to quit before I had to come to you. That's a sign that you know yourself and your limitations, and are willing to take responsibility for your decisions."

I want to say that actually, I don't know myself. That I had thought I could do this job, right up until yesterday. That my nerves are completely shot, and last night I had been so relieved that my shrink thought I should quit—but although I know I have no choice, there is a little niggling voice that says, you could do it if you set your mind to it, you could have done this job but you failed again because of lack of will power, your weakness, and because you didn't want it enough. That is my father's voice, a little worm of sound that burrows and burrows through my head.

"There's no need for you to drive today," Jane says firmly. "I don't expect two weeks notice when you are quitting for—medical reasons." My mother must have told her I was seeing a psychologist. It's too much. I slump in my chair.

"Joan," she says, not unkindly, "you're a smart girl. You just have to find your niche."

I can't believe it. I can't believe that my mother told Jane my private business in order to get me fired and that Jane is giving me career advice, after having just let me go. It's surreal and unnatural, as though someone shattered a bottle of champagne over my head and then offered me a glass to celebrate. Jane turns back to her papers.

"Don't worry. Since it was your probationary period, we don't have to put 'fired' or 'quit' on your record. We have just mutually agreed that it didn't work out. Soon, I'm sure, you'll find something more suited to your—something that suits you."

I drive home, the truth percolating slowly through my brain. I feel so utterly exhausted, as though I have had the wind knocked out of me, by falling on the sidewalk, and am too stunned to even feel humiliated. The steering wheel is heavy in my hands as I turn into the driveway, which slopes down toward the garage door in the basement. The sun is only just reaching above the horizon, and the grass is dewy, in the blue twilight.

I turn off the engine and sit there. The garage door is a pale blue-grey wall, set in the concrete of the basement wall. I feel the slope of the driveway beneath me, as though I've come to a halt before the entrance of the underworld.

The starlings began their vigorous chatter in the pear tree on the front lawn even before I left for the day and continue now. It occurs to me that they are completely absorbed by their own world, full of its daily drama and intrigues and over-arced by the changing seasons. They are, for the most part, indifferent to the world of human beings. We live parallel lives, our societies closed to one another, our passions and concerns never intersecting. And I am flooded with loneliness for a tribe I never had—it didn't exist, even in the dark reaches of time, long before my ancestors were ever imagined into being.

Eighteen

My father is knocking on my bedroom door. "Joan!" he says in a low voice. I roll over on to my stomach. My hair feels soft and sticks out all over my head. I bury my face in the pillow. His voice rises with irritation and anxiety. "Joan you're late for work...Are you ill?"

It is no use pretending.

"I quit my job, Dad," I say in what I hope is a calm and reasonable tone of voice. My father is quiet for a moment, then I hear his exasperated breath and imagine him pulling his hand over his face, over his stubbly chin.

"Joan," he says. There is nothing more. I hear him walk back down the hall in his slippers.

It is noon before I get the courage to come out to the kitchen in my bathrobe. My father is outside raking leaves. He reminds me of a steam engine, raking and puffing on his pipe. It is clear he is thinking, as he claws again and again at the grass with the rake. But it is an obsessive rather than a meditative action, as though he is trying to claw something up from the ground, over and over. He glances over at the kitchen window and sees me sitting at the table with a cup of tea. Under his bloodshot gaze, I feel five years old. He turns his back on me and continues his work.

I am weak and shaky, everything around me stark, as though I have a hangover.

My mother comes home for lunch. She takes a quick look at my face and my father outside in the yard and puts down her bags of groceries.

"I brought you something," she says shyly. I look down at my tea. "Sesame candy from the Chinese store," she says. My stomach rumbles. "Come on, have some," my mother coaxes, and sits down next to me, putting one arm around my shoulders. I stand up.

"Mom," I say evenly, as I have been practicing in bed all morning. Her hand slides down my back, to my waist. "I quit my job," I say, moving away from her. She looks startled—her eyes widen slightly and her lips part. She looks young enough to be my sister. Her hair is still black and falls to her shoulders, framing her lovely face.

"I couldn't handle the stress," I say, a hollow place in my chest where my strength should be. "You didn't have to call Jane. I quit on my own." My voice rises and thins, like the last of the air escaping a balloon. "I am quite capable of quitting a job on my own," I say. And then although I hate myself for it, I sit down in the next chair over and cry, my tears running and dripping off the end of my nose and my ear lobes. My mother takes my face in her hands. She is crying too.

"Oh, Joan," is all she says.

The screen door opens. My father lets it bang closed behind him. I look up at him silhouetted against the light, taking off his work gloves. For a moment, he stands there, while his eyes adjust. His face is perturbed and worried as he sits down beside us.

I feel my mother mustering herself to say something, but before she can, I blurt, "I know you're upset Dad, but I couldn't do it. I had to quit." I tell him how it felt to drive the bus, like a marsupial with a crowd of five-year-olds hanging off my underbelly. My parents look slightly bewildered.

"Stress," I say. My mother nods in sympathy but my father's face clouds over.

"Joan, any job is going to involve stress," he says, controlling his voice. I wipe my nose and look down at my hands, which are slightly blotchy. My mother is about to come to my defence, but before she can, I shoot back.

"Then maybe there is no job I can do," I say. My father's eyebrows draw together. He stands up, walks down the hall to his study, and closes the door behind him.

My mother sits back in her chair. She is struggling to find words to say to me, but her guilt holds her back. She was the one, after all, who pointed out the job driving a school bus to me. And then, she was the one who had called Jane to get me fired—so she is in no position to comfort or advise me. I suddenly realize that my mother feels impotent. After all her efforts to control the situation, and ensure a happy ending, she has come up empty-handed, again. I turn away from her and go back to my bedroom.

A few days later, I go to see Dr. Bard. He welcomes me into his office with a tragicomic expression, his arms opened wide. I bypass the hug and sit on his orange couch, overcome with gloom. Dr. Bard looks concerned, but keeps quiet, waiting for me to speak. Eventually, the uncomfortable silence leads me to say what is going through my mind.

"I don't know what will become of me." Dr. Bard's forehead wrinkles. "I don't know what will become of me," I say again, shaking my head. Surprisingly, I only feel a kind of wonder that I am still floating, still alive on this open sea. But really, what will become of me?

Nineteen

On the first day of school, I felt a cloud of anxiety looming inside me. My mother had put my school clothes to one side—a white blouse, blue skirt and blue knee socks. She had taken the skirt up, pinning it first while I stood on the deacon's bench, then hemming it on her sewing machine.

"You're taller but not so tall," said my mother, eyebrows contracted in concentration, holding a row of pins between her lips. Standing on the bench, I could see the dust on the leaves of plants and the book shelves. Everything looked different, from where I stood now.

"There," sighed my mother, "all done." She made me try the hemmed skirt on. I stood in the middle of the living room, while my mother disappeared into the kitchen. Feeling abandoned, I almost sat down on the carpet—but soon my mother appeared again, holding a lunch box. I couldn't breathe. It had a picture of Scooby-Doo on it. I watched Scooby-Doo on Saturday mornings, before my parents woke up. I didn't even know my mother knew I liked Scooby-Doo. I looked up in wonder at my mother smiling down at me, benevolent as the sun.

The next day, my mother woke me up early. My father was sitting in the kitchen reading the paper when I came in wearing my pyjamas. He smiled down at me.

"How's my little school girl?" he said. I wasn't sure how I felt. Excited. Anxious. I wasn't used to having my parents' eyes on me, full of expectation.

My mother drove me to school the very first day. She took my hand and walked into the schoolyard. There were more children than I had ever seen before in my life. I clung to my mother's arm. We walked past all the girls playing hopscotch and jumping rope, and the boys playing dodge ball, and went right through the front doors.

Somehow my mother knew where to go. We walked down a long hall, with rooms full of wooden desks on either side. Finally at the end of the hall, we entered a room where the desks were smaller and a dark-haired woman with lips red as a fire engine sat reading from a ledger at a big desk in front of the classroom. She looked up as we entered the room, and smiled. It was a sharp, pointed smile.

My mother walked me up in front of the dark-haired woman's desk. "Hi Miss McCartney. This is Joan, Joan Simpson," my mother said. "She's in your class this year." I felt my mother's hand steering me toward Miss McCartney, who put out her own hand by way of greeting. I shook it, and both my mother and Miss McCartney laughed. Miss McCartney sounded like a billy goat.

As the grown-ups talked, I looked around the room. There were some plants by the open windows, a shelf of books, a globe and enormous chalkboards. There were some words written on them in chalk.

"She's never been to pre-school," my mother was telling Miss McCartney, in an apologetic voice. "She can tie her shoes though."

Miss McCartney looked down at me. I felt as though her teacher's gaze would pierce me through. I couldn't speak, but hid behind my mother.

"You're the first little girl in my class," Miss McCartney said. "Can you be in charge of watering the plants?" I peered around my mother's leg. Miss McCartney's smile was sticky, like a peanut butter sandwich. I nodded. I knew how to water plants.

My mother left while I was dousing the geraniums, the only flowering plant in the dozen that lined Miss McCartney's classroom windows. When I turned around, I caught sight of my mother's back and the door to the classroom closing behind her. My eyes began to well. But before tears appeared, the door opened again and another mother entered with a child in tow, and another mother and child after her. I didn't want to cry in front of them. The little girl and boy, mousy-haired and pale, stared at me. The children both seemed to be about my age, but Miss McCartney didn't give them jobs like mine. Instead she sent them to look at books.

What I remembered from the first day of school was the smell of the chalk, the redness of the geraniums, and the sun slanting in the window. When my parents asked me what I did that day I would barely say. I had sat at my desk with papers and scissors and practised cutting and colouring, and printing the first letter of my name, but it was all mixed up together. The thing that stood out like the sound of a bell in still air was that I had a job, watering the plants. The other children were a nameless mass.

Soon, I would learn to differentiate among them. But for the most part, except for Priscilla, I kept to myself. Priscilla had brown hair and a pointed face that reminded me of a fox. She copied everything that I did and when it was too complicated for her she would throw a tantrum, crying and screaming at the top of her lungs. Miss McCartney would place her on a mat in the corner of the room until she stopped, lying there, looking up at the ceiling, with snot and tears dripping down the side of her face. I was shocked by these outbursts, and made anxious by the thought that whatever I did, if Priscilla couldn't follow, it would lead to disaster.

One day, without warning, Priscilla decided she was fast friends with another little girl, Candy. They turned their backs on me, whispering and giggling to each other and ignoring my attempts to join them. My heart fluttered painfully, like a broken bird, but I was also relieved. I kept to myself, dutifully doing all the tasks set out for the children by Miss McCartney and not trying to impinge on any of the groups that had begun to form, quite naturally, among the children in my class. It felt safe. I was used to being alone.

Twenty

I t was to be my first birthday party. Edna was invited, and the Jamiesons and the Tulleys, and of course my grandparents. No children—but that was alright because the thought of having to play with other children I didn't know made me anxious. Grandma Wong wore her gold bracelet and locket, and my grandfather, a button-down shirt and tie, which he kept trying to adjust, as though it were choking him. Finally, after he inadvertently dipped it in a bowl of chip dip, my mother suggested he take it off, and he gratefully complied, stuffing it into his pocket.

Edna wore a cream-coloured dress with little black flowers and leaves and vines, and, beaming, presented my mother with a poppy seed cake. Dr. Jamieson and his wife brought a bottle of wine and, for me, wrapped in pink tissue paper, a picture book with Mickey and Minnie Mouse. The Tulleys, who were very old, brought a bouquet of flowers from their garden. I looked up at their faces, a patchwork of wrinkles. They smiled and blinked at me behind their glasses.

I wondered how it happened, that people became so old. Did they go to bed young and wake up with grey hair and a cane, or did old age sneak up on a person slowly? Either way, it was treacherous. Old age could steal your life from you and fill your heart with grief. I knew I couldn't halt the advancing desert, but I made up my mind to try to hide from it, in the shadow of my parents.

Mrs. Tulley reached down to hand me a few packages of seeds, the loose skin at her neck jiggling like a turkey wattle. I shrank from the touch of Mrs. Tulley's liver-spotted hand, but I took the seeds. There were carrots, radishes and nasturtiums. The Tulleys seemed embarrassed by their unorthodox gift—my mother had neglected to invite them till the last minute, and no doubt they'd had no time to buy a present—but I was pleased to have the beginnings of my very own garden. Though I spent a lot of time playing in the yard with my mother, she had not thought to teach me to grow my own plants, and I had never asked her. Timid in the face of my mother's self-absorption, I preferred to tag along behind her, like a balloon attached to her wrist, a little floating world appended to her own.

Edna bent down and pinched my cheek. "So you are five today, little one." Then she corrected herself. "You are not so little now, are you?" She wagged her finger at me as though she were not the one who had made the mistake, and sat down heavily in my mother's easy chair. Dr. Jamieson held her elbow to steady her, and Edna blushed and giggled when he touched her. Mrs. Jamieson seemed barely there—she was thin and proper and never spoke very much. I always thought her severe, the way she wore her hair pulled back from her forehead and swept into a bun. But later, looking back, I would imagine her smiling gently, almost beatifically, over all of us.

"So you have started school, Joan?" Mrs. Jamieson asked, in a soft, gravelly voice. I nodded, and felt my cheeks grow hot. School made me anxious. The other children were so loud and rambunctious, especially the boys.

My father was in a sombre mood. He had heard the news of Chairman Mao's death a couple hours before the guests arrived, on the kitchen radio, while he was drinking tea. I was at the kitchen counter on a stool, helping my mother make the birthday cake, stirring cocoa into the dry ingredients. It made me think of a sand castle, the way the flour peaked in the middle of the bowl, with the darker swirl of cocoa through it, almost like a liquid. My mother, who had been beating the eggs for the cake, stopped and held the fork dripping over the bowl. My father held his head in his hands. I caught the name "Chairman Mao" and the words, "the Chinese people are in mourning." I knew that when it was dark in China it was daytime in Canada—my mother had explained how the earth turned in a circle, as though it were showing off a new dress to the sun, and that the earth was always dark on the side not facing the sun—but I didn't know why my father looked so distraught, just because it was morning in China.

"Chairman Mao is dead," the radio said.

My spoon clattered to the counter.

"Ssshhh," said my mother. My face felt red and hot, as though my core were melting.

Chairman Mao was something like Santa Claus. My father had told me about him many times—how he marched a long way through the countryside, fighting the people who wanted to hurt the Chinese, and punishing the bad landlords. He had saved China, my father said. Chairman Mao looked round-faced and grandfatherly and he had a bump on his chin like Edna. He liked the colour red, like Santa, and had a yellow star on his flag. I liked to listen to my father's Chinese records. My mother would look cross and read the newspaper, but my father would sing along rousingly to songs like "The East is Red." He and I would march around the living room, our arms swinging and knees high. As the end of it, my father, slightly damp from sweat, would say to me, "Imagine the Long March, when Chairman Mao and his men went up and down mountains for years and years. All they had to eat was rice and pickled cabbage." I couldn't imagine. I had tasted pickled cabbage and it was awful. My little legs and arms were tired from half an hour of marching—how did Chairman Mao do it?

And now he was dead—like the bird I had found in the garden.

"Don't touch it," my mother had said. Its little legs were flexed and its claws curled, its feathers were tattered, and its body sunken. "It must have been the Tulleys' cat that killed it, and left it under the tree in our front yard," my mother said. She buried it there, with her garden spade, and I laid two sticks, crossed like a "t" on top. My mother looked surprised.

"Who taught you to make a cross?" she asked, sharply. My face felt hot. I didn't know why I felt embarrassed. I had seen crosses on coffins, maybe on television. Maybe it was an old photo Edna had—it showed a coffin draped in black with a white cross, and many people standing around it, looking sad and solemn. It was what you do when a person dies.

Then my mother smiled and brushed the hair off my forehead. Her hand felt cool, and she looked beautiful, with her own hair neatly contained in a kerchief, and slightly pink lipsticked lips.

"The cross is a good idea," she declared. "It will let the other birds know that one of their own is buried here." I felt relieved. Yes, it was good that the other birds should know so they could visit their dead cousin from time to time.

Chairman Mao was dead but Santa Claus never died—my father had told me that when he was a boy, Santa brought him presents at Christmas, and when his father was a boy, Santa brought him presents too.

A few days after my birthday party I asked my mother how old Santa Claus was. She was busy studying her book-keeping books.

"Hmm?" she asked, looking up absently. I felt suddenly stricken.

"Is Santa going to die?" I asked. My mother's eyebrows shot

up, and she laid aside her books.

"Whatever gave you that idea?" she asked. I told her that Santa must be very, very old. She smiled. "Santa will never die," she said. "He is magic."

I had always thought Chairman Mao was magic too. He was strong as a horse, smarter than a fox, and fierce as a bear, my father said. He was also kind, and took care of the poor children of China. But now he was dead.

As my father digested the news of Mao's death, he lit a candle and placed in on the mantelpiece, in front of a little photo of a painting of Chairman Mao. When the party guests arrived, no one seemed to notice it. But Edna, who hadn't been in the living room before (she and my mother always drank tea in the kitchen), came across it as she inspected the knickknacks on the mantelpiece. She stopped short in front of the candle and photo of Chairman Mao, and I felt her harden. But she didn't say a word. Instead she took her seat in the easy chair.

When it was time for cake, I blew out the candles. My mother had placed them in a clump in the middle, so that it would be easier for me.

"We must drink a toast to Joan," Dr. Jamieson said. He lifted his glass. "To Joan," he said, "who is five years old today. May she grow up to be as lovely as her mother."

My mother blushed, of course, and the others laughed, the way grownups do when they are drinking and having a good time. My grandparents, looking stiff and sitting together quietly on the sofa, smiled slightly.

My father, who was not laughing, stood up, raising his glass. Everyone smiled at him expectantly.

"To Chairman Mao..." he said. His face contorted. My grandparents stiffened, clutching their wine glasses. Their faces looked like masks but their shoulders wilted a little, as if they were resigned to this moment. My mother looked startled, and embarrassed, as my father mastered himself. With heartfelt emotion, he declared: "May Chairman Mao live on in the hearts of the Chinese people."

The Tulleys and the Jamiesons lifted their glasses politely, while my grandparents sat stock-still. And Edna, one arm across her chest, raised her glass to her lips. I looked up at her from my seat on the living room carpet, holding the seeds the Tulleys gave me.

"The old goat," Edna muttered.

Twenty-one

It's the morning after I quit work, and it's my birthday. I'm turning thirty, and I feel like an empty oil drum, rusting away in the junkyard, weeds growing up around it. My mother has baked a cake, and I ice it while she is at work, with the icing she made for me.

"Joan, you choose the icing colour," she says before she leaves for work. "The food colouring is in the cupboard over the sink."

At thirty, I am still living at home with my parents, no job, no boyfriend. My biggest responsibility is to choose the colour of the icing on my birthday cake. Inside, I am dark and shaky, like a copper beech, rattling its leaves in the breeze.

The usual candle burns on the mantelpiece. My father is outside in the yard, digging around in the garden, and I watch the candle flicker, its thin column of smoke rising to the living room ceiling. My father has lit a candle on my birthday every year since I turned five—but the candle is not for me. It's for the glorious leader of the Chinese people, Chairman Mao, who died on September 9, 1976, the day I turned five years old.

Like the very first candle, this year's is white, the colour of mourning in China, and short—one of the emergency candles my mother buys and keeps in the kitchen drawer with the flashlight and extra batteries. It was probably the only candle my father could find—my parents are not given to romantic evenings, and my mother doesn't like the smell of them, ever since her Chinese wedding.

I don't know how long I've been sitting here. There's no reason for me to get up, no reason to stay where I am. There's nothing in the world that needs me—so I sit and watch the candle on the mantelpiece burn down.

Later, my parents and I gather around the kitchen table, eating pizza, with another candle lit between us. My father has made a salad of tomatoes from the garden with fresh mint. It is standard on my birthday—always a candle for Chairman Mao and something made from tomatoes for me, in remembrance of my mother picking tomatoes when she felt her water break. I've never really liked tomatoes, but they are the colour of happiness—my grandmother believed that was important.

My father pours us some red wine. Although I don't usually drink (it makes my face turn red and hot, so I think I may be allergic), I am on my second glass.

"Your father and I have been talking," my mother says. I am now on high alert, chewing through the doughy crust of pizza. "We thought perhaps you'd like to take a course, since you're not working now." She smiles at me, somewhat apologetically.

My father wipes his mouth on a napkin and nods at me. "We'd pay for it," he says, eyes averted.

I look down at my pizza, as though to consult it, as a soothsayer might the entrails of some unfortunate sacrifice. A course? My mother is rambling on about something, how well I did at English in school, why don't I think about that, or maybe I could try journalism. She always talks fast when she's nervous, and her small nose, banded by summer freckles, flares slightly at the nostrils.

My father clears his throat and shifts in his chair. "I was thinking of something more like a secretarial course, or perhaps something in business administration," he says. "There are some good, practical courses at the community college, and you don't have to study for four years to achieve a diploma, which doesn't give you any hard skills anyway."

My parents have clearly covered this ground before and agreed to disagree. They don't look at one another.

"It's your choice," my mother says, and my father nods.

It always surprises me that my father, with his university education, is the more pragmatic one when it comes to work and preparing for a career. Of course, years ago when I graduated from high school, he had hoped I'd go to university, but he seems to have long since given up that idea. Whereas for my mother, a university education has the glamorous sheen that is only apparent to those who never had the opportunity to go.

To me university is a place of misery, where I floundered in the few courses I took after high school, and where I never felt confident enough to make friends. I would climb the steps to the back of the class, which sloped upward from the front where the professor stood. From my vantage point above the crowd, I could sometimes only barely hear the professor, and I never asked or answered questions. If I was lucky, I would be beside an open window, and could hear the birds chirping in the trees or the vines covering the brickwork. Their leaves blazed red in the fall and the birds seemed to be busy among them, perhaps eating berries. They squabbled and shrieked, sounding so much more vivid and purposeful than I felt at that moment.

One day I brought the crust of my sandwich and placed it on the sill of the open window, hoping a bird would perch there. It was my first-year English class, and I hadn't read the text on which the prof, a thirty-something bearded man with a British accent and the standard tweed jacket with leather elbow patches, was lecturing. I watched him out of the corner of my eye, pacing up and down in front of the class, and stopping occasionally, throwing out his arms, as if astonished by something he had just said, to a ripple of laughter from the students.

A bird appeared on the window sill—a young starling, an

iridescent sheen glossing its brown head and speckled breast. It pecked at the crust and looked at me, as if I were going to snatch the bread away from it. Then to my surprise, instead of flying away with it, the bird came toward me, even hopping down onto the classroom floor. My chest fluttered with anxiety and I felt my face grow hot. The starling flurried into the air above me and landed on the steps in the middle of the rows of desks, the bread crust in his beak. A few students gasped, and began to laugh, turning sideways in their seats to look.

The prof quipped, "A bird in the class is worth two in the bush," and advanced toward the starling, a book in his hand. The starling looked at him quizzically, as though sizing him up, then flew over his head and zigzagged around the class like a bat, to the shrieks of young women, until finally it found the classroom door and disappeared into the hallway. The prof, looking slightly shaken, closed the door, saying, "Well, I suppose this is a bird course after all. We can only hope the poor creature will find its way through the halls of higher learning and escape unscathed, as ignorant as before."

That was the day I stopped going to English class, though I continued with psychology and calculus. There were hundreds of students in the psychology class and the exams were multiple choice. It was easy to remain anonymous, and, arriving late, I avoided having to interact with the other students. Calculus was a bit trickier, since the class was not as big and the subject more challenging. I actually enjoyed it, becoming absorbed in the numbers and formulas, contemplating the mysterious laws that governed them. Like my mother, I was able to lose myself in the forest of mathematics—so pure and beautiful and unassailable, like a stand of virgin pine on a craggy cliff.

But I am not at all keen to go back to university. I look at my mother across the table, and my father, stirring milk into his coffee, the pizza box lying greasy and now useless, to one side. My mother cuts the birthday cake—no birthday candles, just a big *30* emblazoned in purple icing on a green background, reminding me of a football jersey. A course? There is nothing I want to learn that would get me a job I would want to have. I need to think about how to break this news to my parents, as well as to come up with a plan of some kind that will satisfy them.

My mother pushes a university calendar toward me. "All the courses are in here," she says, as though I don't know what a university calendar is for. "You'll have to decide soon if you want to get into the fall courses—they've started already." She picks up the pizza box and stuffs it in the broom closet where she keeps recyclables. It's final—the end of my birthday supper.

My father doesn't provide me with a calendar for the community college. "It's all online," he says, his slice of cake remaining untouched in front of him. He picks it up in a paper napkin and proceeds to his study. I watch his thin, slightly stooped shoulders as he disappears into the darkness of the hallway. From behind, he looks so much like my mother's father, long dead from heartache.

My mother sits down again across from me, looking tired. It seems strange and sad that throughout my childhood, I tagged along after her, hoping for her undivided attention— and now that I am an adult child, needing to break away from my parents, she has begun to focus on me. But she really isn't focussed on me, I realize. Her eyes have a glassy look, and she is gazing over my shoulder, as though there is someone else—a small girl with black hair and slanted eyes, who stands behind me, looking at her. My mother's five-year-old self. I am merely someone who sits between them, keeping them—uneasy and ambivalent—from one another.

Twenty-two

American sign language...Personal Care Worker...Photography...Welding. I scroll through the whole online calendar of the community college and don't find anything that I can picture myself doing. Why is that, I wonder. Some people know from childhood exactly what they're aiming for, and never veer from that course. Others seem to have an epiphany somewhere along the way, and discover a passion for something that they hadn't even dreamed of, such as phlebotomy or arboriculture. But I have drifted along like so much flotsam, never finding the shore, and never certain what it will look like once I arrive there.

And I do believe I was put here for something; we all are. My parents wrinkle their noses at the mention of God but I have always felt there was something inside us that needed to be expressed—the way an acorn is destined to grow into a tree, we contain within us the seed of what we are meant to become.

It was Edna who first gave me that idea. Sometime not long after my fifth birthday, she asked me what I wanted to be when I grew up. It was a matter-of-fact enough question. She was kneading bread at the Jamiesons' kitchen counter, and my mother was drinking the Christmas tree drink at the kitchen table. They had talked about my mother's bookkeeping courses, which she had almost completed. My mother looked happy and that made me happy, as I nibbled a dry cracker with a cup of juice in my hand.

"What you want to be when you grow up, Joan?" Edna asked over her shoulder. With juice dribbling down my chin and the circular mark from the plastic cup around my mouth, I replied hesitantly, "A fairy." Fairies never died, like Tinkerbell. My mother smiled and put her hand to her mouth. Edna turned and looked at me.

"A fairy?" She addressed my mother. "I know what a fairy is," she said, her face contracted with concern.

My mother laughed. "Edna, not that kind of fairy. She means a little creature with wings—magic. Imaginary."

Edna's face softened with relief. "Oh. Ah," she exclaimed. "That is what a fairy is. I see." She bent over me with her floury hands. "Joan has big fantasy," she said, gently pinching my cheek. "Maybe she will be artist." I felt suddenly brave enough to pipe up that I would be a fairy and an artist and also an astronaut, but Edna was speaking to my mother about other things.

"So—you think maybe you get good job now you study bookkeeping?" she asked, briskly stretching the dough and doubling it back on itself. My mother nodded modestly, but she was brimming. Edna mused, her strong hands never leaving the dough, "Yes, it is good for woman to know something, to do something. My husband"—it was the first time I had heard Edna mention her husband—"he didn't want a wife more educated than him. So he marry me, before I go to training school. I want learn sewing but he say I know enough. Now I am ignorant old woman." Edna shook her head. "All I can is cooking, cleaning, baby-sit. I can sew but only normal thing—not special."

My mother's eyes were sympathetic. I realized that she and Edna shared something between them that I did not yet understand. I had always looked on Edna with awe. She was so big and strong and capable, she could cook anything, and she also crocheted; she had given my mother a plastic doll in a pink crocheted dress that stood inside a toilet roll on the toilet tank. She could sing songs with words I didn't know, she knew how to clean stains off anything, and she could cut beautiful snowflakes out of paper to tape to my window at Christmas time.

Edna turned to me, her eyes sharp. "Little one," she said, plopping a little piece of dough in front of me so I could make my own small loaf, "in Canada, you grow up strong and free," she said, quoting the national anthem slightly out of context. "You be what you want. Look inside your heart and you will see, what God has planted for you. Before you born, he put seed there. This is—how you say—desire, what you want in life. This seed grows and grows, and what you make in the world is like a tree. The kind of tree is depends on God. He make a maple or oak, or he make you want be a nurse or teacher. You can even be fairy if you want." She made a face at my mother, who laughed. I took the dough in my hands. It was warm and squishy, and reminded me of something newborn, without bones.

On the way home, I could tell my mother was ruminating on what Edna had said. She grasped my hand, which felt small and hot and damp in hers, and said nothing as we crossed the Jamiesons' lawn to ours. I was imagining a little oak tree growing from my heart. It made me anxious, thinking that a tree could suddenly sprout, its roots and branches growing out of my nose, mouth and ears, and its trunk bursting through the top of my head.

It gave me comfort to hold my mother's hand and to know that she didn't have a tree growing out of her, nor did my father. When we reached our house, my mother hesitated at the front door, as if she was undecided about going in. As if she were a visitor, and it wasn't even her house.

Twenty-three

In the days following my first day of school, nothing changed—the boys and girls still screeched around the playground in the late summer sun. I sat down in a corner of the sandbox, and began to build a mountain. I took two sticks and made a cross on top, and then scattered the sand everywhere, so no one could ask what I'd done.

One day was like another in Miss McCartney's class. Her voice droned on and on, and I tried to follow the thread of her instructions amidst the chaos in the classroom. Sometimes I caught Miss McCartney frowning at me. I didn't know why Miss McCartney didn't like me, but it made me anxious. It was one thing for the other children to ignore me, but another to think my teacher disapproved.

After school was my favourite time. Edna looked after me on school day afternoons, since my mother had taken a bookkeeping job at the supermarket. I'd sit at the Jamiesons' kitchen table, chatting with Edna, who was always busy baking something—brownies or raisin bread and sometimes poppy seed cake. I'd kept quiet all day at school, and so it was like a dam bursting—I told Edna every single story I could think of about my classmates and what I thought of them and what we had learned that day.

Edna looked down at me with crinkly eyes, nodding and pushing toward me a piece of whatever she had baked, along with a glass of milk. Sometimes Edna looked like she would cry. At those times she would turn away to the sink where there was always a dish or two needing washing. I never knew what it was that made Edna sad, but it didn't last long. Edna would scoop me out of my chair and dance a few steps with me.

"You must learn Hungarian dance," Edna insisted. "I teach you karikazo." But that never lasted either. Edna, who looked so light on her feet, was out of breath before she could show me more than a few steps.

After my snack, Edna often put me to work, shining the silverware or dusting the bookshelves. I liked both jobs, because the silverware had beautiful patterns of twining flowers on their handles, and on the bookshelf, there was a pile of *National Geographic* magazines full of astounding photographs. I sat on the floor, twirling the feather duster in one hand and flipping pages with the other—polar bears, the Grand Canyon and African tribes who wore disks in their lips and stretched the necks of their women with coiled necklaces. The women's breasts did not look like my mother's, which I imagined were small and rounded under her short-sleeved sweaters. They were more like triangles—or fish, firm and pointed, dangling over their chests as though they had just caught them in the river.

Edna looked over my shoulder, then bent down to grab the magazine off my lap. Edna *tsk tsked* and, as my face grew hot and red, she told me, "You no look at those dirty pictures. They no for children." She was blushing herself. "You come to the kitchen—I let you water plants."

That night I dreamed of African women, with babies on their backs, bending over a well, their breasts swaying. I was at the bottom of the well, and it was dark but I wasn't wet at all. The women didn't seem to see me—they lowered a bucket to draw water and I knew I could grab hold of the bucket, and they would pull me to the surface. But somehow, I didn't want to be discovered—it was cool and comfortable in the dark and I felt safe. The women would never know I was there and I could contemplate them in secret and overhear their gossip. There was something comforting about that, even though I realized the bottom of a well was no place for a child.

My first report card didn't reveal much. "Joan is tidy and obedient," my mother read, squinting at Miss McCartney's handwriting, which was sharp and dark, not fine and spidery like Edna's. "She could benefit from interacting more with the other children." I didn't know what that meant. My mother frowned, then smiled. "But with her quiet ways she is a plea-sure to have in my class." A pleasure, I thought. Sounded like treasure. My mother squeezed my cheek.

"That's a fine report card," she said. My father, glancing at it after supper between the sports section and the evening news, agreed.

I liked the things Edna taught me better than the ones I learned in school. How to thread a needle, how to wash a window so that it didn't streak, how to gently dust houseplants. In the years to follow, when I had homework, Edna had no time for book learning but she was a teacher of great distinc-tion when it came to home economics. Before I was eight, I knew how to sew on a button, knead bread and bake cookies.

"You will be a wonderful woman who know how to make house," said Edna, beaming. "Many men will knock on your door, when you are older."

I didn't care. I just wanted to sit with Edna in a patch of sunlight at the Jamiesons' kitchen table, and for the afternoon to never end.

If the school year was a blur, summer vacation stood out like a brilliant butterfly. It was the golden time between one school grade and another, spent with Edna and a teenage babysitter, who took me to the pool and sat sunbathing and doing her nails during my swimming lessons. Afterward, I splashed around in my water wings, until the day near the end of my fifth summer when a wasp frightened me and I plunged without wings into the shallow end. I opened my eyes underwater for the first time, to the glistening turquoise of the pool. There was no sound, except for the fizzing of myriad tiny bubbles coming from my nose and lips.

I was fascinated by the idea that I had stumbled by accident on the secret world of fish and mermaids, the only one they ever knew. Maybe if I held my breath long enough, I could become one of them. But to my disappointment, every time, I found myself on the surface again, lungs bursting.

Summertime was also when Edna made jam and fruit preserves. I would find her in the kitchen with a pot bubbling on the stove, and mounds of strawberries in bowls on the kitchen table. Did Edna pick them, I wondered? Once a summer, my parents would take me to a U-pick farm in the Valley. I would pick a quart or two then sit lazily between the rows, eating the warm berries off the plant. But Edna was capable of picking twenty quarts at one sitting, I was sure of it.

As if reading my mind Edna said, "They bought them, no pick. From a man with truck on side of the highway. They buy everything! And they want me make jam." Edna shook her head and smiled.

I didn't blame them. "Your jam is nice," I told Edna, who smiled again and placed a bowl of strawberries, covered in real whipped cream, in front of me. That was Edna, and that was summertime.

August was when my anxiety began. The thought of school loomed like a truck barrelling along the highway toward me, and I couldn't jump out if its way. Though I had proved myself not to be a fish or a mermaid, I felt like an underwater creature next to my classmates. The speed at which I thought and moved was sluggish compared to them, as though I were living in liquid. My parents had no idea about my social awkwardness, and neither did Edna. Although I wanted very much to be able to confide in someone, I didn't want to disappoint them. All my parents and Edna knew was that I was quiet, but doing well at my schoolwork.

The monotony of school days was prickled with dark moments when Edna's attention shifted to other children. Edna never had much money in her life but she was generous. She gave out cookies like gold coins to any kid who came door-to-door fundraising, and though she never pledged a dollar, they all left the Jamiesons' door feeling special. I felt a terrible abandonment when Edna would answer the door after school and hold her cheery conversations with the very children that I kept at a distance.

Edna also gave away clothes and books to the Salvation Army, and glass bottles to panhandlers so they could exchange them for money. It occurred to me after Edna died that she was always trying to atone for something by giving stuff away.

"Here. You like this doll?" she asked when I was very young. "It's Hungarian folk doll. You take," she said, pressing it into my arms. I looked up at my mother's face to see if I had permission but my mother looked confused. Even then I felt that there was something not quite right about Edna's gift-giving.

Edna started working for the Jamiesons in the 1950s and stuck it out until the late '80s. Dr. Jamieson had been her GP and their conversation came around to the fact that he and his wife needed someone to clean and cook for them. Edna, already besotted by Dr. Jamieson's gentle touch, said she would gladly do so. Dr. Jamieson, who knew Edna to be strong and healthy as a horse, took her up on the offer. She would live in the Jamiesons' mother-in-law suite in the basement and keep house for him and his wife.

Edna could have found better jobs, I thought when I was old enough to ponder such things. Edna had many skills. Like my grandmother, Edna could have been a seamstress, or like my grandfather, a cook in a restaurant. She could have made twice what the Jamiesons paid her. But she stuck with them. It could have been because of her attachment to Dr. Jamieson, or it could have been that she felt the need to be constant, to show her loyalty to someone. They were a little like family to Edna, after all.

As was I, I suppose. I even looked a little like Edna. I have her considerable frame, her small dark eyes and strong features, though my hair is brown, not black like Edna's. I liked to imagine that we were related, that Edna was in fact a great aunt of mine. I didn't know anything then about DNA, but I hoped that somehow across the continents that separated our forebears, there had been a moment where lightning had mixed our blood together.

Edna was still a teenager when she came from Hungary. In Canada, though at first she was still young and attractive in a buxom sort of way, she never married. She had quite a few dates over the years with men from her church, but they never amounted to much. I saw them pick her up at the Jamiesons' to take her out for dinner, but that only happened once or twice and then there were no more visits from that particular gentleman.

"Too much men," she said with a sniff and a wave of her hand as we sat topping and tailing beans. "They all want something."

Edna was a devout Catholic. She went to Mass every Sunday morning, wearing a smart hat and her good dress with panty hose. When she came home, she looked as though she'd been caught in a spring rain. Her face was damp and rosy and her eyes full of stars.

"My sins are washed away. I am clean," she told me with a dreamy smile. I looked up at her with wide eyes. Was there a shower in Edna's church where people could wash themselves? I knew it wouldn't be an ordinary shower because I had tried the shower at home after I stole cough drops from my parents' bathroom cupboard. It didn't make me feel any less guilty, just wet.

I never asked Edna about Hungary and the life she left behind. Once I asked whether Edna flew on an airplane to come to Canada and Edna laughed.

"No plane, little one. Boat. Big boat." Her forehead crinkled, remembering. I could feel it was not the time to ask more questions. When I was old enough to wonder how it was that Edna ended up here all alone, and what she had left behind, I felt there must be a melancholy tale involved. I knew somehow that this was a story that could not be pried loose from Edna without opening a river of hurt.

So from the beginning, I invented stories for Edna. Her mother beat her, so she stowed away on a ship carrying meat-ball soup and poppy seed cake to come all the way to Canada. Her sisters were jealous, and they tied Edna up and put her in a sack to drop off the edge of a pier, but instead she landed in a small boat which was ferrying people and goods out to a visiting steamliner, and ended up in cargo. In all the stories I invented about Edna, she landed in a pile of food, so she wouldn't go hungry, and her ocean voyage resulted in her fattening up to her present size. I didn't know for some years that "Hungary" was not a place where everyone was hungry, nor that it was a landlocked country and that Edna would have had to spend days on a riverboat before she ever reached the sea.

Edna had been part of my life almost since before my life began. Her story and the story of my mother and father, and of me are surely intertwined, even if our DNA is not. According to my mother, when Edna first met her, soon after she and my father moved into the bungalow next door to the Jamiesons, Edna was on her way to church. My mother was seven months pregnant, down on her knees, weeding the garden. Edna was wearing a very striking hat with a long peacock feather, and looked, my mother thought, a little bit like the Queen Mother. She raised her hand with the trowel and called, "Hi Mrs. Jamieson!" Edna stopped in her tracks. Holding her purse in two hands, Edna walked with quick little steps toward her, beet red and breathless.

"Hi there," said my mother again. "Mrs. Jamieson?" Edna tittered and put her hand over her mouth. My mother thought at first that there was something wrong with her neighbour's head. Edna bent toward her as though to whisper a secret.

"My name is Edna," she said. "No Mrs. Jamieson. I clean Mrs. Jamieson's house." My mother took off a glove and offered her hand to Edna.

"Lucky Mrs. Jamieson," she sighed.

Edna smiled. "When you have baby?" she asked.

"Soon, I hope," my mother replied. "It's going to be a long summer."

Edna touched her shoulder. "You call me. When you have baby. I bring you something." My mother gazed up at her. Edna waved at her with a finger, straightened up and pushed her hat to a jaunty angle. "I must go to church," she said, and crossed herself, right there on the front lawn, startling my mother. "May you have healthy baby," she said. My mother smiled and watched Edna teeter on her pointy shoes toward the bus stop.

When I was born, Edna visited us at home. She brought with her a pot of chicken soup. My mother tasted it and startled. It was seasoned with ginger root. "This is the way my mother makes it," she said. "How did you know?"

Edna winked at her. "Edna knows something," she said and smiled. "I have Chinese friend. She tell me this is what a woman need after baby." My mother's mouth hung open. A more thoughtful gift Edna could not have given her, even though leftovers from her mother's pot of soup were still sitting in the fridge.

Edna glanced over at the bassinet. "So....?" she asked.

My mother nodded. "It's a girl," she said. She didn't know if it was normal or not but she barely cared. Mostly she felt exhausted and wanted to stay in bed. "Joan."

Edna moved quietly around the couch to see me sleeping, my hands curled in little fists. She gazed down for a long time, but didn't touch me.

"Go ahead," my mother said, nodding toward the bassinet. "You can pick her up."

Edna's face shifted. "No," she said meekly. "I let her sleep." She smiled, but her eyes were sad. "You rest. I go home."

When my grandmother came the next day and saw there was a full pot of soup in the fridge she frowned.

"You no eat my soup?" she demanded.

"No Ma," my mother said weakly, "we ate all your soup. Edna gave me another pot." Her mother looked unconvinced. "Edna, the Jamiesons' housekeeper. She has a Chinese friend." My grandmother's eyebrows shot up. "Edna's from... somewhere over in Eastern Europe. Hungary, I think." My mother felt completely drained.

"What does Hungary woman know about Chinese food?" my grandmother demanded. My mother closed her eyes. Grandma Wong stood and looked at her for a moment. When my mother began to snore, my grandmother took a spoon from the kitchen counter and dipped it into the pot of soup. She sampled it cold, and her eyes opened wide at the taste of ginger.

My grandmother stood over the bassinet. She brushed my cheek as I slept, and provoked an involuntary smile. A bubble appeared between my lips. My grandmother's mouth was tender but firm.

"You a Chinese baby," she said. "At least half. Half Chinese is better than nothing."

Twenty-four

It's been difficult to stay at home, since I quit my job as a school bus driver. My mother's anxious gaze and my father's frown of disappointment are always before me. I shut myself in my bedroom for the first couple days but since then I've taken myself out of the house, away from my parents. The place I always end up is the nursing home where Edna lives.

It's a sprawling flat-roofed building with lots of windows, but as a rule, most of the curtains and blinds are drawn. Edna has her own room, on the corner facing the meadow and the road that leads from the home down to the main road. She likes to sit in her wheelchair and watch the birds. They come to the bird feeder that is stuck on her window with a plastic suction cup. They bicker and squawk at one another, vying for a space to cling to the feeder, and that always makes Edna laugh.

"They are like little men. Look how they fight," she says.

Edna likes small things these days. Bingo on Thursday nights in the dining hall. She usually wins something, a box of Kleenex or a little bottle of shampoo, and she shows me proudly when I come to visit her on the weekend. She likes the routine of mealtime, even though she complains about the cooking. The soft desserts, she takes from her tray to save for a snack—yogurt, Jell-O, and her favourite, pistachio pudding. She can eat them even after she takes out her dentures and her gums are bare as a newborn baby's.

I show up at her door on a Friday, carrying a bag of sunflower seeds to refill the feeder. Edna smiles politely when she sees me, and says graciously, "Please, come in." I know she doesn't recognize me.

"Hi Edna, it's Joan," I say in a loud voice. Her eyes look cloudy and unfocussed, their rims red as though she's been crying.

"Please, sit down," she says, smiling, her mouth gooey from lunch. No one has come to wipe her chin.

"Edna," I say softly. She seems to startle. "It's me, Joan." Edna's face scrunches up like a ball of paper, and she begins to cry. "Edna, it's alright," I say, taking her hand. My touch seems to bring her back to herself. She snuffles into a Kleenex and looks up at me.

"Joan," she says, and holds my hand.

We sit quietly for a moment. It is always heart-wrenching, when she comes to from her confusion—it hurts both of us every time, and it is almost a relief when she drifts back into semi-consciousness. I take the napkin from her tray.

"May I?" I ask, gesturing toward her mouth. She points her chin toward me. I dab at it, and her mouth and cheeks as though I am a makeup artist. Then I look into her eyes and try to smile.

"Joan, where am I?" she asks, bewildered. Just as I have every time I come to visit her, I say, "You're at Mount Pleasant." I leave the words "Nursing Home" off the end. "Mount Pleasant" is such a wonderful name, reassuring and at the same time lofty.

"Ah…" she says, her eyes widening. I wheel her to the window and exclaim, "Look what a lovely view you have, from Mount Pleasant. You can see the birds and the sky, and over there," I say, pointing to the harbour, "you can see the ocean." It isn't a lie, and it seems to make Edna happy for awhile.

"It is like my home," she says. I never know whether she means Hungary on the River Danube, where she has not lived for more than fifty years, or the last room she occupied, where, in a little space between the refrigerator and the door, there was a window that looked over the harbour.

Edna and I play Go Fish and Crazy Eights when she is lucid. Sometimes I ask her to teach me to knit. Her fingers are swollen with arthritis but she shows me how to hold the needles and cast on and off, to knit and purl. I always forget what I have learned, and Edna forgets she has taught me, so it is a perfect activity to repeat.

When Edna teaches me, she seems very like her old self. She crosses her arms across her big bosom and watches me struggle, then she clucks with her tongue and takes it upon herself to show me the right way to do it. Even with her gnarly old hands, she makes the needles click and fly. I admire her work and then make a stab at finishing a row of stitches. She examines it, shakes her head and says, "No, no, this is too tight," or too loose, or she remarks that I have dropped a stitch—and then she briskly fixes it, and presents it to me, triumphantly, eyes shining.

"This is good knitting. You knit like a man," she says, laughing her old, hearty laugh, and I laugh too for the joy of hearing that sound, like sunshine pouring gold into a dark place.

Twenty-five

I am working my way haphazardly through my past, trying to piece together a story. It seems I am always working too tightly or loosely, and end up pulling it apart, looking for the dropped stitch, the split fibre, the place where I've lost the pattern and wandered too far from the truth.

When I was eleven, a girl in my class at school was having a birthday party, and I wasn't invited. At lunch the girls sat in a clump of desks, eating their sandwiches and talking about the party to come, while I sat silently among them, mortified. They didn't bother to include me, nor did they hide the fact that I wasn't invited to the party. Miserable, and without anyone else to talk to, I told my mother that evening what had happened. She didn't say much but stroked my hand in sympathy, and I could feel her pained eyes follow me as I went to my room.

The next day at school, Elsa came up to my desk. Tossing her brown hair over her shoulder, head held high, she placed an envelope on the corner of my desk.

"Joan," she began, bending forward confidentially, kindly, I thought. "You can come to my party. It's on Saturday at three p.m." She gave a small smile, and turned away. The other girls stared at me, also smiling, but I sensed the hardness in them.

When Saturday came, I took pre-emptive measures against anxiety and put a package of cough drops in my purse. My mother brushed the hair from my eyes and grinned.

"My, don't you look nice," she said as I climbed from the car in a pink dress that she had added a panel to, because I was too big for it. I had just begun to notice that most other girls were a few sizes smaller than me, and the added panel was a source of misery. But my mother had also done my hair the night before with big curlers, and I liked the way the curls bounced on my shoulders as I walked.

When I rang the doorbell, Elsa's mother answered. She smiled kindly, her face under her makeup slightly pocked and her short brown hair stiff with spray, and invited me in.

"The girls are downstairs," she said, ushering me to the steps. As I slowly descended, careful not to trip over my sandals, which had a slight heel, I could hear my classmates giggling and whispering. When I reached the bottom, I saw that they were sitting in a circle on the floor, with the lights turned off and candles lit. I mustered a smile.

"Happy birthday, Elsa," I said, thrusting the gift-wrapped package, complete with curly pink bow, in her direction. She took it and smiled, her small mouth dark red with lipstick that made me think of Bing cherries.

"Thank you Joan," she said primly, and placed it behind her on the sofa.

The girls were sitting around a Ouija board. Elsa explained that each of them could ask a question and placing their hand lightly on the pointer, the spirit world would guide it to spell out the answer to her question. Elsa said that since it was her birthday, she would also put her hand on the pointer.

Elsa's best friend Margaret, a tall thin girl with red curls and freckles, demanded to ask the first question. She closed her eyes and breathed in.

"Does Billy like me?" Billy was a boy in our class, a good athlete, stolid, dark-haired and not very smart. Margaret and Elsa put their hands on the pointer, which began to slide slowly about the board. *N-O*—Margaret's mouth trembled. But the pointer continued *T-Y-E-T*. Margaret's small eyes widened, and the girls around her squealed. My mouth hung open. Elsa looked smug.

"Who else has a question?" she asked.

Diane, a small, dark-haired girl, put her hand forward. She was an excellent gymnast, which gave her a certain popularity at school, although she was quiet and shy.

"I want to ask something," she declared. She took a small breath, sucking in her cheeks. "Will my parents get back together?" The girls sat quietly, looking down at the board. Diane's parents had separated at the end of the school year last year and her father had moved to an apartment across town.

Her hand trembled on the pointer. Elsa, looking slightly embarrassed, rested her fingers lightly on the pointer and it began to move. It seemed to be travelling across the board without landing on any letters. Finally it settled on the letter *U*. Diane held her breath. "*N-K-N-O-W-N*," Elsa read, "unknown." She looked shocked, and Diane exhaled, her shoulders sloping.

There was a darkness in the air above the Ouija board—we all felt it. The candles flickered slightly, as though a flock of crows were beating their wings, trying to alight. Margaret began to laugh, a high, thin, hysterical sound—she clamped her hand over her mouth, but couldn't seem to stop. I noticed for the first time that the basement was drafty, damp and there was a smell of mildew. Elsa looked tired, her hair limp. Margaret's laughter had turned into a cough.

Elsa's mother came part way down the stairs.

"Girls, are you alright? Margaret, come upstairs for a drink of water. In fact you can all come up—it's time for cake," she said.

We were all glad to leave the dank room and the Ouija board behind. Elsa blew out the candles and everyone ran for the stairs, almost in a panic. We were too old to be afraid of the dark, but no one wanted to be the last to leave.

As I reached the bottom of the stairs, I tripped on my sandals and fell against the bottom few steps, and against Margaret, who was clambering just ahead of me.

Margaret screeched as she fell. Her eyes glittered as she turned on me.

"You cow," she hissed.

"I'm sorry—I didn't mean to," I stammered. The dark was growing behind me, like smoke billowing up from a fire. Margaret reached the top of the staircase and slammed the door shut. In desperation, I pounded against it with my fists.

"Let me out," I pleaded. In a loud voice, Margaret declared, "That cow tried to climb over me. She made me fall and bruise my hand. Look..." I imagined her holding up her bony, freckled hand for the other girls to see.

Elsa sighed dramatically—then said, in a voice just loud enough for me to hear, but not her mother, "I wouldn't have invited her, but her mother called mine, and asked if she could come. Mum made me give her an invitation." One of the girls gasped and another snickered.

I felt as though I'd been plunged into the winter ocean. The girls' giggles and knowing voices dimmed and trailed away from the door, which slowly swung open, as though there had been no resistance in the first place. The kitchen was empty—everyone was in the dining room. I stood at the top of the stairs, darkness pooling behind me. The kitchen floor, white and blue linoleum, shone dully, and in the late afternoon light, the white walls were cold and grey.

I stood at the threshold a long time, not wanting to step into the kitchen, though the darkness sucked at my back. Then Elsa's mother came into the kitchen to look for me. She smiled kindly, wiping her hands on the apron she wore over her jeans, and said, "Joan, your ice cream's getting cold. Come eat." Pretending that I had just then climbed the stairs, I smiled back, and brushed past her into the dining room.

The girls were gossiping and squealing with laughter at the table under the light of the crystal chandelier and hardly glanced at me when I entered. It was as though I was the only one who remembered what had happened just moments before.

The light from the chandelier made the room look hollow, and dark in the corners, and the girls' faces had dark shadows under their eyes. Their laughter seemed insane—a raucous, meaningless noise that covered nothing.

I sat down where there was an empty chair and a piece of cake, the ice cream already softening at the edges, like a snow bank in the sun. Though I didn't feel like eating it, I did, because it let me avert my eyes from my betrayers. They paid me no more heed than if I were a stone, whistling and chattering amongst themselves, like a pack of hungry starlings.

When my mother picked me up from the party, I slouched in the back seat sucking hard on a cough drop so I wouldn't have to talk. If she could tell I was angry and hurt she didn't ask why. I avoided her attempts to make eye contact with me in the rear view mirror. I was as bitter as the cough drop dissolving on my tongue. My mother had started to take an interest in my life, at last. Perhaps she felt guilty for previous omissions, or maybe I had reached an age where my mother felt we could talk as friends, confidantes. But I didn't want her friendship or her secrets. I just wanted to be left alone, and not to have my mother calling my schoolmates' parents to wrangle party invitations.

That evening, after supper, I did my math homework at the kitchen table while my mother washed the dishes at the kitchen window. Whenever she got her hands in soapy water, she would begin to daydream. I watched as she wiped the same plate, in a circular motion, over and over again. Tonight, her brow furrowed and her mouth was a worried frown.

The bitter taste of the afternoon's humiliation finally left my mouth, and as my mother struggled with herself at the kitchen sink, my resolve to hate her dissolved like soap.

"Mum," I called to her. She looked as though she'd been submerged in a dream, and I had pulled her from it. "Mum, shall I dry?" My mother tried to smile at me, but the corners of her unruly mouth tugged downward and her face was a flower of disappointment. "Next time, darling." she said, and turned back to her dishes.

Twenty-six

I like to take Edna outside, into the wind and sun. I push her chair along the gravel roadway but she never complains about the bumps. Across the road from the nursing home is a meadow that is never mown, full of goldenrod and asters and any number of other weeds. Edna looks into the long grasses, which bend in the wind and where birds and butterflies hunt for seeds and flowers. Beyond it in the distance is the harbour, but that's not what holds Edna's attention when we are outside. It is the lives of the creatures close at hand that captivate her.

I think that I will bring her a bird book next time I visit. I will bring a butterfly net, and some binoculars. It feels like I need to do something, anything, to prolong and expand this moment. Edna sits peacefully, a serene look on her face. She wouldn't know what to do with a bird book or binoculars. I push her to the end of the gravel, and think, as I always do, what if I just kept going?

But instead of continuing down the paved hill, I turn the chair around. Edna is blissfully unaware that I have contemplated her escape. Even at her most distressed, it never seems to occur to her to try to make a break for it, and that hurts me. She is strangely passive, not like the old Edna, who could make light work of mounds of laundry and cook up huge batches of jam and a turkey dinner at the same time. When the nurses or personal care workers come to look in on her during my visits, they say what a sweetie Edna is, and pat her on the shoulder. In other words, she doesn't give them much trouble. Edna smiles back, indulgently perhaps, but her eyes are blank.

When I leave, I tell Edna I will finish the knitting at home. That I will come to see her next week, and that I will bring her something to read. Sometimes she bursts into tears and clings to me and begs me not to go—those are terrible times. And at others, she looks at me with bright, blank eyes and clasps my hand, and thanks me for coming. Those are the times I feel like crying and beating the floor with my hands. But today she is asleep in her wheelchair, smiling slightly with her head tipped sideways on her shoulder and a slick of drool like a snail's trail sliding down her chin. I tell her I love her and that even though she has to live in this awful place, she is still my Edna.

When I feel my hands on the steering wheel, my whole body seems to vibrate, the way it does after a loud rock concert when you've been standing in front of the speakers. My hands and feet work calmly, seeming to know exactly what to do, while inside me, everything is jumbled.

My cough drops are on the dash. I take one, and then another before reaching home. Inside the sweetness is bitterness, and inside the bitterness is a white place, where everything disappears. It is a small journey to take, away from the pain of life, into the heart of nothingness. You don't need a driver's license. You can go there anytime and you always know the way back.

Twenty-seven

I am sitting outside in a lawn chair, reading in the late September sun. My mother is shopping and my father has gone to the library, so it's only me and my cup of coffee—and my cough drops. Listening to the crickets and watching the last butterfly among the goldenrod, I suck pensively on a cherry Halls. I don't feel anxious, but I'm still in need of its soothing magic. My inner shakiness has been getting worse since I quit my job and now I make sure I always have a roll of Halls nearby, as insurance against total collapse. Seeing Edna at the nursing home usually requires several lozenges and then there is afterwards, when there is no one to turn to who understands my aloneness.

I can still remember a time when cough drops were just for coughs. I hated them as a child, though I had barely tasted them. I would never have imagined that they would become my best friend and comforter. And a means of self-flagellation, a bittersweet punishment for stealing the money to buy them from my mother's purse.

Today I feel detached, and in an almost abstract way, I pity my younger self at the moment when a cough drop replaced human contact and my emotions became bilge water, collecting in the dank underbelly of my life. It wasn't that I consciously wanted to escape from my feelings so much as that I didn't know what to do with them, so I let them drip away in the darkness until I could barely recognize them. Eventually I couldn't even remember what I felt.

I first used a cough drop to forget when I was eight years old, and my grandmother was dying. She had emphysema my mother told me many years later, from my grandfather smoking. I remembered Grandma Wong gasping for breath, lying in the hospital bed with an oxygen mask on. When my mother took me to visit her, I was afraid of the breathing apparatus. My grandmother had always seemed severe and cold, and with the oxygen mask on, she looked alien. But my mother put my hand in my grandmother's hand, which was small and soft, and she squeezed it. It felt like my grandmother, and I smelled the familiar baby powder smell on her wrists.

My mother kept up a brave face when she went to visit the hospital, but as soon as we left my grandmother's room and began walking down the hall, she began to crumble. She held my hand, walking faster and faster toward the elevator. Once inside she took out a handkerchief and blew her nose. The hot tears had already started tracking down her face. She grabbed my hand again and we almost ran to the parking lot. Inside the car, my mother clutched the steering wheel and leaned her head against it and bawled. I sat beside her, unsure of what to do. I chewed the end of my braid, which my mother hated, but she didn't notice me doing it this time.

There was a package of cherry Hall's cough drops on the dash board. I knew they tasted awful but I put one in my mouth. There was the sweet cherry candy flavour, and the bitter medicinal taste. My tongue found the dent in the middle of the cough drop and let the medicine leech on to it. I lost myself in the trance of flavours, while my mouth went numb and the cough drop turned into a sliver of candy. I leaned back in the seat, at peace, while my mother sobbed.

On his fortieth birthday, not long before my grandmother died, my father let me try his cigar and I ended up fainting, face up on the floor in his study. That was also before my mother, in her grief, became a martinet where smoking was concerned. Some days, she would sit, sobbing without tears, at the coffee table in the living room, with a photo album of her parents and herself as a little girl. At first, my father would try, awkwardly and quietly, to comfort her, but she would not be consoled, so after a time he would not even come out of his study. In fact, he would shut the door tightly against the sound of my mother sobbing. At those times I would play quietly in my room, sucking on a cough drop and waiting for my mother to begin to sigh and hiccup, which indicated that she was ready to put her things away and go into the kitchen to make supper or do the dishes.

Early on, I sensed something had gone awry in our home but I couldn't quite put my finger on what. The house seemed sad, even when the drapes were open and the sun came streaming in. There was an underwater feeling, and I almost expected to see schools of fish, darting among the shadows of the living room.

I realize now my mother was grieving the loss of both her parents, whom I know mostly from photos, yellow and sticky, stuck by my mother in a cheap photo album. My grandmother Wei Ying, short and round faced, squinting at the camera on my mother's wedding day. My mother, taller and slimmer, looks tired and resigned and much like a Chinese doll, beside her. Grandpa Wong, lanky and slightly stooped, has his arm around her shoulder. He looks into the camera as if he is trying to see the person who, so many years later, is looking back at him. His dark eyes are strained and searching, but also shiny with happiness and pride, across the great gulf of time that separates us.

I look back at him, his younger self, and I look at my mother, in whose belly I am quietly dividing. To the end of his days, she was precious to him, this daughter who was conceived in a steamship somewhere over the Pacific Ocean. And she is the vessel that carries me, still closed like a fist in her womb, tight as a peony bud. I feel his love for her spill over onto me, surrounding me like a warm bath—and gradually, I feel myself unclench and come loose from my moorings.

There are photos too of the wedding in the school house—swaths of flowers, a red "double happiness" banner over the doorway, with the Chinese characters painted in gold by Mr. Liu, who owned a small restaurant downtown. The backs of so many heads of black hair, looking toward my mother and my father's surrogate, Harold, who also stand with their backs to the camera—only the justice of the peace, a short bespectacled man with brown wisps combed over his balding hairline, is facing the camera. Then there is a photo where Gillian and Harold are half-turned toward the back of the school house, looking as if toward an intruder, someone who has interrupted them. My mother's eyes are dark and she does not smile. It's as though she is about to step on board a ship for a long journey, away from people she knows and loves.

My mother's marriage to my Maoist father did indeed carry her away from her parents. In my imagination, I picture my grandmother standing erect, clutching her handbag in front of her, and my grandfather, much taller, behind her. They are dressed as they were at my fifth birthday, when Mao died. After that, it almost seems as though they were absent from my life at home. My mother would still drive me to visit them, and my grandmother would often feed me little half-moon dumplings, almost transparent enough to see the delicious morsels of pork and crunchy water chestnut inside. But I don't remember them coming to our house after that—perhaps because after the death of Mao, my father no longer bothered to hide his political leanings out of respect for their sensibilities. I remember him, aggrieved, trying to argue with my grandfather about Mao's contributions to China, and my grandfather edging his way to the back door, outside of which he stood and smoked for a long time, looking out over the garden.

After Mao died, the fact that my parents were on diverging paths must have been clear to my grandparents. But it was long before I was born that my parents' spirits turned away from one another; perhaps it was on the very night that I was conceived. The night the tiny specks of my mother's ova and my father's sperm collided, held each other in a death grip and waltzed together in the sloshy warmth of my mother's uterus. When the cells began to divide, and differentiated themselves into the various parts of me—hands, heart, liver— my parents were also dividing away from one another. They didn't know it at first. My mother would repeat the same accusations against Mao and his disastrous policies—the Great Leap Forward and the Cultural Revolution—and my father would counter with his arguments about how Mao saved China from the Japanese and made China a proud nation with its Iron Rice Bowl guaranteeing no one would go hungry from cradle to grave. After awhile, I could see that their hearts weren't in it. Ostensibly they were arguing but in fact they were merely drifting away from one another, like two survivors of a shipwreck on different life rafts, caught in opposing currents. As if somehow they had got it backwards—and they were becoming strangers who knew less and less about one another, after having started as friends.

My Grandma Wong has been dead a long time now, but even her corpse would frown at my father's political proclivities. At her funeral, she looked tiny in her coffin, her face powdered and rouged, sleeping in her silken jacket with the collar buttoned tightly under her chin. That night, I dreamt that she was still alive and that she was angry, banging around the kitchen, slamming pots down on the counter so their lids jumped. I asked her what the matter was and she turned to me with burning eyes.

"Your father," she hissed, "let the birds out." I looked out the window and saw that the tree was bare against the late November sky, except for a half dozen pigeons, the last of a flock which was, at that moment, scattering over the rooftops.

In death, my grandmother was at least as formidable as I always thought her to be in life. My grandfather who, sick at heart, died the same year, six months later, was always the weaker of the two. I imagine him on a galloping horse, trying to catch up to my grandmother in the afterlife. She is being carried over the celestial mountains in a silk-draped litter, serene and never looking back.

Twenty-eight

A t home, I see my parents out in the back garden through the dining room glass door, speaking intently to one another—it is hard to tell whether they are arguing or in agreement. I go to my room and lie down, waiting for the tingling to stop, and fall asleep. When I awake, in the blue shadows of late afternoon, I unravel the knitting that Edna and I had done. Like Penelope's burial shroud for Odysseus, it will never be finished.

Twenty-nine

I never really knew my father's parents. They came to visit only once, when I was five. They were very old and grey, and I imagined that they lived on top of a mountain, where the wind whipped their hair and they herded mountain goats. My father seemed to shrink to a stick figure in their presence, and my mother, though a gracious host, barely said a word, and mostly smiled.

I was playing with blocks at my grandparents' feet, as they sat on the living room couch, and looked up at them—their liver-spotted old hands were frightening, but their faces smiled down at me like the sun. Grandfather Simpson ruffled my hair with his hand.

"Such a good lass. She'll be as pretty as her mother yet," he said, puffing on his pipe. My mother blushed, and I looked up at my grandfather in wonder. How did he know? I felt as light as spun glass.

Grandmother Simpson was soft and reminded me of a rag doll. Even her housedress made me think of Annie, who had long brown yarn hair and button eyes. Annie sat up straight like a soldier at the head of the bed, waiting patiently for me to climb in each night, then dissolved into softness in my arms. Annie was much younger than Grandma, though; maybe Annie was her granddaughter. Maybe, I thought, Annie was my sister! I had never thought much about being an only child but the idea of Annie as my sister seemed to open a chasm of longing, and my eyes felt hot with tears.

As though she could read my mind, my grandmother asked gently, "David, have you and Gilly thought about having more children?"

My mother had returned to the kitchen, to prepare the food. My father was sitting in his easy chair, drinking an awful lot, and he kept having to hop up to go to the bathroom.

Grandfather Simpson said in a loud voice, "Sure, young Joan here might fancy a playmate. How'd you fancy a little brother, eh?" he asked. He leaned down over me, all jovial face and pink cheeks.

"I don't want a brother," I piped up. He leaned back, surprised, and then both my grandparents laughed. My father sipped his Coke, which must have had rum in it, and looked grim. When my mother came from the kitchen with a stack of small plates, Grandfather practically shouted, "Gilly, our Joan says she doesn't want a brother...maybe she'd be happier with a baby sister?" Grandmother patted his arm to try to quiet him, and smiled apologetically.

Just then the doorbell rang, and my mother's parents entered. My father downed the last of his rum and Coke, and jumped up to take their jackets. Grandma Wong had a long silk scarf that she unwound from her neck, unsmiling. Grandpa Wong bobbed his head in a small bow to the Simpsons and extended his hand to Grandfather Simpson. Grandmother Simpson rose from her seat to clasp the hand of Grandma Wong, who smiled back briefly and then sat down in my mother's easy chair.

My father poured drinks for my grandparents, while my mother bustled around bringing food out of the kitchen. Edna had given her some recipes and even loaned her the icing piper to make devilled eggs. I could tell my mother felt

154

proud—she didn't say much but she laid a platter of devilled eggs, surrounded by flower-cut radishes, carefully on the table.

Grandma Wong looked up at her sharply. "What this?" she asked.

"Ah, devilled eggs!" Grandmother Simpson exclaimed. "I have always wanted to try them." She took one in a napkin, and daintily raised it to her mouth. Her eyes widened. "Delicious!" she said delightedly.

My Chinese grandmother looked confused. "Devil eggs?" she asked. I looked up at my mother, eyes wide. Were these eggs from the Devil's chickens?

Grandmother Simpson turned to her, and said, pleasantly and almost conspiratorially "Have you never heard of them? The Americans like them. My nephew lives in South Carolina and his wife Sally makes them all the time." Grandma Wong said nothing, but scooped an egg into her napkin, to inspect it. I held my breath, almost expecting her to tuck it into her purse to take home with her—but she sniffed it, then took a small bite. She didn't spit it out. I let myself exhale.

Grandmother Simpson held out the plate. "Dear, would you like to try a devilled egg? They're quite delicious," she said kindly. I shrank from the offering, into the shins of Grandma Wong, who waved the plate away.

"She no like. She like Chinese eggs." This was not quite true. I didn't like hardboiled eggs of any kind, including those fried with soy sauce that my grandmother cooked for dinner parties. But I didn't contradict Grandma Wong, who had saved me from eating the Devil's eggs.

Grandmother Simpson looked bewildered and slightly hurt. Grandpa Wong, gallant as ever, came to the rescue and chose two devilled eggs from the plate she still held. Grandma Wong's eyes narrowed. Without missing a beat, Grandpa stuffed half an egg into his mouth. His eyes closed.

"Mmm," he said with his mouth full. I was afraid he was going to turn red and fall down from eating the Devil's eggs, but he sat back down in my father's easy chair.

The grandfathers were talking to each other, despite the difficulties with one another's accents, about football and the flight from England, and so on. Grandmother Simpson tried to engage Grandma Wong in a discussion of Chinese food.

"David loves your cooking," she said with a glance sideways to my father as he wandered off to the kitchen. There he stood, looking helpless, while my mother bustled around putting things on a tray for him to take out to the living room. "He never did much like the food I cooked at home," she admitted, with a small sigh. "He was always fussy as a child, never liked potatoes. One day we took him to the Chinese restaurant in York, as an adventure. He didn't want to come home!" Grandma Wong looked slightly mollified.

"Chinese food is best in world," she said, sitting straight-backed in the easy chair. Grandmother Simpson leaned forward to hear her better, but that was all she said.

Mother came out of the kitchen in her pink apron, a plate of coconut squares in her hand. She offered them to the grand-mothers. Grandma Wong waved her hand.

"Too sweet," she said severely. Grandmother Simpson tried to smile.

"Gillian dear, these look scrumptious," she said, helping herself and her husband to one each. My mother put the plate on the table, and cut a square into four pieces. One she gave to me, and one she placed on a napkin for her own mother.

"Ma, taste one," she said. "It's from Mary Lai's recipe. Remember you had one at...the wedding...and you liked them." My British grandparents didn't know about my mother's Chinese wedding to my father's surrogate.

Grandma Wong picked up the piece of square between two

fingers. I stood by the armrest of her chair, thinking she might give it to me.

"Joan," Grandma said, shooing me away. "You no eat more. You getting too fat."

My mother must have seen my look of shock. "Ma, Joan isn't fat. She is just big-boned."

"She looks very plump and healthy," Grandmother Simpson said pleasantly. "I think she takes after you, with her lovely round face and wavy hair," she told Grandma Wong, who blushed, her hands clutching the handle of her purse. Without meaning to, Grandmother Simpson had just complimented and insulted her at the same time.

I felt the same way. I didn't want to look like Grandma Wong, whose small eyes and tight, down-turned mouth made me think of a sea creature, something without mammalian warmth. I wanted to look like my mother, slender and delicate, whose shiny black hair made me think of a doll's that never really needed combing, except for the pleasure of it.

That evening, as I was brushing my teeth in the bathroom with my mother beside me, I looked at our reflection in the mirror. My head was almost as big as my mother's, and my wavy brown hair radiated out on both sides. There were my small eyes and mouth, and big cheeks, next to my mother's shapely cheekbones, almond eyes, and rosy complexion. Could my grandfather be wrong? Was it possible I would not be as pretty as my mother when I grew up?

My mother was tired, her face a mask. She barely glanced at the mirror, except to wipe off some toothpaste spittle.

"Off to bed," she said, wearily.

Thirty

My English grandparents stayed for only a week, and then they were gone, to visit a nephew in New Jersey. I was glad, because then my routine went back to normal. I went to Edna after school until my mother came home from work, and my parents, although they never said anything, seemed relieved. I never saw the Simpsons again. The next year, my grandmother caught flu and died, and my grandfather, broken with grief, moved in with his sister but went downhill fast. Before the year was out my father returned to England a second time for his father's funeral.

I don't remember my father being upset. My parents spoke to each other in hushed tones before he left and again when he returned. I thought about my grandparents being dead, and then I thought about the bird the Tulleys' cat had caught and left under the tree in the yard, and I wondered whether my father had remembered to put a cross on the dirt to mark where my grandparents lay. He told me they had been "cremated" and that meant—my father swallowed before he said this—that their bodies were burnt and that their ashes were contained in a little box. Did it hurt to be cremated, even when you're dead? He didn't show me the box, but I imagined a little parcel tied up in brown paper. I wondered whether it was going through the post office and whether it had been sent to someone, or whether it would just sit there on a shelf. It made me anxious to think it could get lost, and that it might not have a cross on it to let people know there was someone dead inside.

My routine had returned to normal, but Edna had changed. She seemed tired. She said the doctor had discovered she had a disease called diabetes, and that she couldn't eat sweets any longer. How horrible, I thought, looking up at Edna as she bustled around the Jamiesons' kitchen. She looked fine—but then, so had my grandmother, who caught flu and died. Old age was a precarious thing. It was better to stay in the garden of childhood forever than to knock on the door of adulthood. Could I drag my feet and tear my clothes and become unfit to enter that house? But I knew even then that this was not possible, although it wasn't clear to me what would happen if I tried.

One Saturday I awoke from a nap and trundled out to the living room, where my mother was standing, looking out the living room window. There was an ambulance parked in front of the Tulleys' house, and my mother was on the phone.

"Yes Ma, I know. Their daughter is over there with Mrs. Tulley now. She said he fell asleep in his chair and never woke up....uh-huh...She knew he was gone because his pipe fell on the floor and he didn't startle." My mother put her hand to her forehead to brush hair from her eyes. I stood in the hallway watching the red light of the ambulance flashing round and round. It pulsed around the walls of our living room like a race car. "Mrs. Tulley says she will sell the house and give the money to the church. She's going to live with her daughter."

A pot began to boil over on the stove. When my mother turned and saw me standing there, there was dismay and confusion on her face.

"Joan," she said. For a minute I thought my mother was going to kneel and hug me, and I stiffened in preparation—

but she just took my hand and looked into my face. "Joan, Mr. Tulley died today." I knew it already of course, but hearing my mother say it made me anxious that there was something I was supposed to feel. If anything, I felt insecure. As though Death could reach out and pluck anyone from my life without warning. Could my parents die? What about Edna? There was a lump in my throat, and I couldn't speak. Even Chairman Mao, strong as an ox and magic like Santa, had died. I held on to my mother's hand, who squeezed mine back awkwardly.

"Come into the kitchen, sweetheart," she said. "I made some coconut squares. We'll take some to Mrs. Tulley later, but you can have one now."

Thirty-one

The next time I go to visit Edna, she is sitting in her wheel-chair in the spot where I had left her. Her thin hair is still half dark between the grey, but it hasn't been washed, it looks like, since my last visit. Her eyes, however, are bright.

"Joan..." she says in a hoarse voice. I take her hand. She motions to me to bend down so I can hear her. "I have job for you."

I am not very hopeful, but I put my ear next to her mouth. "They need workers here. One woman left yesterday. She work in the kitchen. Now they need someone. You ask," she says, shooing me toward the door.

In the hall there are a few old people tottering or wheeling with nurses, who give me perfunctory smiles. There are a couple hospital beds in the hallway, containing bedridden old people with yellowing skin and sunken cheeks. One woman follows me with her eyes as I pass, and I try to smile but my face feels ghastly and contorted.

The woman at the front desk is on the phone, but she smiles and waves me toward her. "Yes...yes...alright I'll take two. And make sure they have the red bows, I don't want nothing new-fangled this year. That's right...thanks." She hangs up and says, "Ordering Christmas wreaths. I can't believe it's that time already. What can I do you for?"

I look at her bowl of Halloween candy on the counter. "Have one," she offers. I shake my head.

"Edna—I mean Mrs. Szabova—told me you might be hiring?" She looks at me sceptically.

"Are you a nurse?" she asks.

"No, I'm…I heard you might need help in the kitchen."

"Oh yeah that's right," she says. "Our meals come in on trays from the hospital, but we do need someone to prepare snacks, clean, and help with feeding." I think of the woman in the bed in the hall. She looks like she'd need to be spoon-fed. I feel myself panicking and say quickly, "Okay…I can do that." The front desk woman looks uncertain.

"Well, bring in your resume and put it to the attention of Justine Blackwell. That's me," she says, flashing her unnaturally even, slightly stained teeth. "I'm Human Resources."

Edna is snoozing in her wheelchair when I go back to her room, passing by the bedridden woman whose eyes are also, thankfully, closed. I sit in the plush easy chair next to Edna's bed, with the morning sun pouring in, and try to read one of the magazines that are piled on the window ledge. The yellowing headlines with their specious promises—*Firmer thighs in thirty days, How to know if your man is cheating*—seem like messages from another planet. They have nothing to do with this life.

Edna snores loudly, an alien sound. I get up to find her shampoo and see that the toilet has not been flushed, so I flush it. Head and Shoulders. Oil of Olay. I grab them and fill a plastic tub under the bathroom sink with warm water. When I come back out, Edna is wide awake and looking right at me. Her eyes seem almost black and her lips are trembling.

"Hi Edna." I say.

"Why you leave me?" she whines piteously.

I am confused. "I—I didn't leave you Edna, I just went to ask Justine about the job you told me about, in the kitchen."

She doesn't seem to hear me. "I stand here in the rain one

hour and you no come," she accuses me. My mouth falls open. She begins to mumble something in Hungarian. Then she bursts out angrily, "You treat me worse than a dog."

My heart splits. Is she talking to me, or to someone she thinks I am? In the past she has sometimes failed to recognize me but she has never mistaken me for someone else.

Her eyes are closed but tears seep out and down her cheeks. I don't know what to do. I start to make crooning sounds, like the pigeons that sleep on the roof of the house across the street from where my grandparents used to live. Then I walk behind her with the tub of warm water and place it on the bed, and wrap a towel around her shoulders. I take a sponge and begin to gently wet her hair and to smooth her forehead and face, erasing the trail of tears left on her cheeks. Then I shampoo her hair as she sits, calmly now, her head tipped back over the back of the wheelchair.

When I was young, Edna would let me brush her hair. It was grey even then, and wiry, but when the brush went through it, it became soft and smooth. Then Edna would brush my hair, as I sat in the kitchen, and sometimes, if I had a headache or if I was upset about something she would massage my temples and my scalp. It felt better than a cup of hot chocolate or a warm bath. Does Edna remember those days?

"Ahh..." Edna groans and shivers. I take the towel from her shoulders and rub her hair with it, until it is almost dry. Edna doesn't use a blow dryer because her curls would become a frizzy mess, and she doesn't like the hot air against her skin.

I sit on the bed beside her. "Edna do you want me to brush your hair?" I ask her. She doesn't answer. She used to let me brush her hair to humour me, but all she ever did herself was to fluff it with her fingers.

"Do you want to look in the mirror?" I try again, but she speaks softly to herself in Hungarian and seems to be gazing, not outward, but at some interior landscape. Her eyes are muted, her voice distant and melodious, as though she is a girl, walking along some mountain trail and singing the songs of her past.

The next day I take my resume to Mount Pleasant Nursing Home. There is a girl at the desk, not Justine, so I leave it with her, and go up the hall toward Edna's room. There are the sounds of a barbershop quartet, coming from behind the folding accordion partition that screens off the lunchroom. No old people in the halls today; perhaps they are all at the concert.

At Edna's door, I look in and see that she is again asleep in her chair. I wonder how uncomfortable it would be to sleep sitting up—she must be very tired. She looks almost cherubic, her face soft and pink, and her breathing gentle. I don't have the heart to disturb her, so I turn back down the hall. The barber shoppers are crooning something I vaguely recognize—a mournful, muffled sound. For some reason I imagine them underwater, arms around each other's shoulders, bubbles rising from their throats, like fish. They look sad, and their music is drowned out by the sound of applause, which is only rain on the surface of the water.

Thirty-two

Now that I am again jobless, I have plenty of time to think about how things might have been different, if only I had followed my father's advice. When I was a child, sitting in the leather chair in my father's study and swinging my feet, he told me to study what I was interested in, and to stop banging the chair legs with my heels. For that reason, his advice seemed to come with an admonishing tone, and to do what I was interested in was not the open door that it might have been to someone less neurotic than me.

As I sit with my cup of tea in my parents' kitchen, I wonder how no one saw how far off track my life would be when I turned thirty. It's true I didn't follow my father's advice, nor Edna's. But of course, advice is wasted on the young—in that I was once a typical sixteen-year-old.

The subject of what I would do with my life never came up with my mother, until I graduated from high school. Today, my mother is probably the last person whose advice I would take, but surprisingly, of the people close to me, it was she who sensed that my trajectory to adulthood might not be typical. That my unhappiness might be as natural to me as weeds, growing in the places where flowers had been planted.

When I graduated from high school, my mother took me out for cheesecake. As we sat across from one another with a candle glowing between us, my mother stressed the importance of having skills and earning my own income. She leaned toward me earnestly, as though her message were secret and urgent.

"You're so bright, Joan," she whispered, nodding her head. "You'll find a good job, and that's important, even if..." Her voice trailed off, and as if distracted, she looked away and wiped her mouth with her napkin. I imagined she was thinking, even if you marry a man who can provide for you. My mother, I imagined, found that idea as far-fetched as I did—marriage was just not something I had given any thought to, and for some reason, although it was hard to put my finger on why, it seemed almost as much an impossibility as flying to the moon.

Edna, however, had other ideas, and other advice. After I graduated from high school, I sat in the Jamiesons' kitchen with Edna, who still kept a bottle of gin under her sink. With a flourish, Edna poured a shot glass to let me try it. Going down, it burned my throat with a cool fire and left the taste of pine needles on my breath. I didn't like it but I wasn't about to tell Edna.

Edna put her arm around my shoulders and squeezed.

"You are no more child," she said proudly. "Look at you," she demanded, pressing my cheeks with her hands. "You grow up. You soon be driving. Then we go to Valley and pick straw-berries, apples, pears. You go to university and become doctor, like...like Dr. Jamieson," she said, reddening.

A doctor? It was the way of most Chinese-Canadian fami-lies—so many parents wanted their children to be doctors, that sometimes there were two or three in one family. My parents would probably have been secretly happy for me to become one too—but they didn't push.

I had a pleasantly warm feeling after drinking the gin. I sat topping and tailing string beans, while Edna looked solemn, wiping her hands on her apron and sitting her plump self down in the chair opposite.

"Joan, you are grown up now. I want tell you something." She took a piece of paper out of her pocket and squinted at it. I was drinking tea and eating apple cake, and I swallowed hard when Edna looked at me, silver glinting from her eyes in the grey afternoon light. No one could scare me like Edna.

"Number one: you too old not to listen to your mama and papa now. You listen what they say. They love you." Edna had caught me off guard. Wasn't now the time I should stop listening to my parents and think for myself? She continued, "Number two: you study hard and go to college; education is most precious thing, more than gold. Only grace of God is better. Number three: You drive carefully. No drink and drive." I smiled at her. Edna regarded me severely.

"Number four: You only let a boy touch you here," she said, pointing to her torso, "above the waist. No below, if you want respect." I gaped at her. "And five. It is most important." I waited. Edna blotted the corner of her mouth and then her eyes with a handkerchief.

"You must listen to what your heart says. It is like a bird, speaking its own language. But it is talking to you. And you must listen." I felt confused, but I nodded solemnly. Edna sighed. "You are a smart girl. But you no understand everything."

Edna got up to fetch a load of laundry for ironing. For the first time I noticed her rub her knees as though to take the stiffness out of them. She asked about some of the neighbourhood boys as she ironed.

"What do you think about that Ricky?" she demanded. Ricky Hauser was a good-looking young man, polite and cheerful, which were at the top of Edna's list of priorities. He still had a paper route, which is how Edna knew him—he'd deliver the paper to the door instead of throwing it from the street, and, tossing his shiny mop of long hair, he'd give her his million-dollar smile. He also spent more time smoking pot outside the school than he did going to class, and I always thought he had the paper route so he'd know who was away, and so he could case out homes to break into, but I didn't tell Edna that.

"What about that Hugh, his father is a lawyer," she said. The steaming iron seemed to draw in its breath. Hugh was the president of the student union. He had a multi-year plan to become a lawyer, marry an unsuspecting, professional female and become a millionaire. Hugh was in my math class, and behind his calculating ways there was a blank cruelty that frightened me so much that I couldn't look at him without shrivelling.

Boys, generally, were alien. They roughhoused, swore and had no compunction about hurting one another. In elementary school, I kept quiet and stayed away from them. Although the girls were catty, they were at least familiar. For their part, the boys more or less ignored me, and everything worked out so that I was comfortably miserable. I had a few short-lived and secret crushes on boys who were athletic, moderately intelligent and polite to me, but I always knew there was something impossible, even outlandish about my fantasies. Junior high was a teary blur and in high school, I found myself emotionally stunted in a forest of teenagers rapidly reaching adulthood. There was no way I could catch up, and my self-consciousness was acute to the point of freakishness.

Edna had no idea about any of this. I stirred a sugar cube morosely around in the little cup of strong black coffee Edna gave me.

"You just shy, sweetie," Edna said, hugging me so hard I felt like some kind of folding chair. "You meet a nice boy one day."

So I had. Once out of the bleak barren of my school years, I met some nice boys—men—but one way or another, those meetings came to nothing. I was not quite sure why, except that by the end of each relationship, I would find them looking at me strangely, as though they couldn't quite put a finger on what was wrong with me.

That night in bed I thought about how I had never noticed Edna growing older. When I was a child, Edna had seemed old, and that was more than ten years ago. If anything, she seemed younger now. I thought how it would be if Edna were actually growing younger, and some day we became the same age. How old would we both be then? Would we be friends? I imagined us walking on opposite sides of the same street. I was window-shopping, and caught a glimpse of Edna's reflection. I stopped and waved but Edna, in her housedress, didn't notice. She was walking briskly, as though in time to some fierce music, in the opposite direction.

Thirty-three

I arrive at Mount Pleasant Nursing Home for my first day of work in the kitchen and find paramedics carrying Edna out on a stretcher. Her lips are blue and her face looks pale and swollen. My stomach feels the way it does when the elevator stops—as though it is just floating up inside me. I tell the paramedics that I know her, that she has no family here, that they can call me, and I touch her hand—it's cold. I keep talking as the paramedics load her into the ambulance, asking where they're taking her, what will happen to her things. She's from Hungary, I say, she lived there many years ago, but she's been here all the time since then, she's Canadian, she never got the chance to study, to have children or to go on a cruise or even a bus tour...I talk fast, and keep talking, as though a litany of Edna's life is the only way to stop what is happening from happening. The ambulance pulls away from the curb. I follow on foot for a way, waving and running. I shout, "She doesn't wear makeup—only lipstick. She likes Bartok. She likes to knit..." I tell them everything I can think of, everything I know about Edna. Everything that will let them know who she is to me. I watch the ambulance go until I can no longer see its lights flashing, reflecting off the cars and windows it passes, my Edna inside, silent. She is meek and mild in death as she never was in life.

They'll take her to the funeral home, and someone will wash her hair for her, and put lipstick on her blue lips. Perhaps she will be touched more lovingly by strangers in these final days than she has been by staff over the past few years at the nursing home. I stand outside and hope she won't be cold, lying in the half-open coffin. She should have brought a sweater. Will they remember to take her dentures out? She'll be lonely, lying there in the night with no one to talk to. For the first time in weeks I take out my cherry Halls and put one in my mouth. It tastes sweet and bitter, soothing. But I have to spit it out because my stomach begins to heave.

Justine comes out when I start running after the ambulance. She puts her hand on my back and holds my arm as I bend over and vomit. She rubs my back with a practiced hand.

"It's alright darling," she says in a gentle but matter-of-fact voice. "She lived a long life. A good life. And now she's gone." I know that Justine knows nothing about Edna but that her words are nevertheless true. A long life, and a good life. Edna worked hard, never complained, squeezed what she could out of every moment. And now she's gone. My Edna.

I go home and go to bed, in the middle of the afternoon. My father is out in the garden, and turns when he hears me in the house but I don't wave or go to tell him why I am home early. Banging open the door, I take off my sneakers and throw them against the wall. I figure I'll let him think I've quit again or that I got fired on my very first day of work.

That night I dream I am a fish. Among the shadows of a dark pool, I dart back and forth, keeping always out of the patches of sunlight. Suddenly a hand appears from above and takes hold of my tail. I struggle to free myself as I'm brought to the surface, thrashing back and forth. As I churn the water, my fins turn into arms and I am swimming in a lane at the swimming pool. Edna, in a pink flowered bathing cap, and bulging out of a one-piece bathing suit, stands on the diving block at the end of the lane, stopwatch in hand. As I touch the wall and look up, she clicks the stop watch, smiling down at me beatifically.

I don't know what to do, now that Edna's gone. I feel awkward and paralyzed, as though I have lost the use of my arms and legs. Edna wouldn't understand. She would say, Joan, it's life. You keep going. Just the way Edna did, when she lost one of the loves of her life.

Many years ago, when I was gloomily making my way through high school, Dr. Jamieson keeled over from a stroke and Mrs. Jamieson told Edna she would be bringing her niece to live with her and that Edna's services would no longer be needed. Edna had no time to grieve. She put her clothes and rags and brushes into two grocery bags, and took the bus to the Catholic church across town. She said she would clean the church, and keep house for Father Daniel if he would give her a little room in the rectory and let her eat meals in the kitchen. It was an offer Father Daniel couldn't refuse since the young woman who had been doing chores for him had just left due to her delicate condition.

What a stroke of luck, for Edna. But she mourned Dr. Jamieson, whom she had coveted in secret. This I didn't find out till much later at the nursing home, when Edna was beginning to be addled with dementia and called out his name, wild with lamentation, and cursed his wife in her own language. I held Edna's hand and she turned to me, surprised, as though she had just woken up.

"Don't listen to me," she said, putting her hands over her face, as though she were going to start sobbing. But she only took a long, quavery breath. "Dr. Jamieson never touch me. He never look at me. Only—fantasy," she said. She looked at me with small, bright eyes. "An old woman must dream something, so no boring...boring kills you, quicker than the heart attack."

Thirty-four

I wake up the day after Edna dies, and I don't know what to do, so I go to work. Justine gives me a tour of the kitchen. There's a woman, dark-skinned and rail-thin, mopping the floor.

"This is Eloise," Justine says. "You two will be working together." Eloise glances at me, smiling quickly then putting her head down, and goes on mopping. She has a long slender neck like a gazelle and big brown eyes in her slender face.

I notice that she is wearing a hairnet over her fuzzy black hair, and put a hand to my own.

"That's right, you'll need a hairnet," Justine says. "Eloise, could you fetch one from the supply closet? Actually, take Joan with you so she knows where it is." Eloise dips her head, like a pigeon, I think.

Eloise walks briskly down the hall, with me trailing behind. I feel miserable. Eloise stops at the wide door across the hall from where Edna used to be. It is all I can do not to burst into Edna's room. There are people inside, wearing hairnets and nurse uniforms, wiping down the plastic mattress. I feel in my pocket for my cough drops. They are there, in their reassuring oblong package.

Eloise beckons inside the supply closet. "Here," she says smiling, "you hairnet." It's then I realize that Eloise is not from around here. I can't place her accent exactly, but I think it must be an African one. Eloise's skin is as black as molasses.

I pull the hairnet on. What would Edna think, I wonder. I must look like one of the women from the grocery store deli.

"Does it look okay?" I ask. Eloise laughs, the sound a burbling brook.

"Yes," she says, smiling shyly, her brown eyes wide. She pokes one finger at me, "*Jolie*."

I doubt that. Tears gather behind my eyes. Edna had been the last person to say I looked pretty, the day I wore barrettes in my hair and a pair of earrings. I plan to dress up for the funeral, but clearly, it won't matter much to Edna, I think flatly.

On the way back to the kitchen, Eloise points to the washrooms. "We clean," she says. I nod. Eloise makes a face. "Not nice," she says, shaking her head, then laughing. I smile.

Justine is checking her watch when the two of us reach the kitchen. "Eloise," she says, a tad severely. Eloise's face is quick with worry. "Did you remember that snack was supposed to be a boiled egg this morning?" Eloise shakes her head then nods. Justine sighs and turned to me.

"She's a hard worker," Justine says, "But her English..." she shrugs her shoulders. "Maybe you can help with that?" I don't see why not. "Eloise will tell you what needs doing for snack. After that you can each take a washroom. I put the eggs on to boil so you'll have them for this afternoon."

When Justine leaves, Eloise takes my hand in her dark and slender one.

"I no cook *oeufs*," she says. "Now we must yogurt and fruit." Eloise waves a finger at me the way Edna used to. Her palm is light pink. "Eloise," she says, and throws up her hands. "*Oeufs*, Wed-nes-days."

Eloise reaches for the tub of yogurt in the fridge. She motions to me to set out the bowls on several large trays. Then she mimes opening a tin of fruit with a can opener. I sigh internally. This job is going to be more of a challenge than I thought.

At ten-thirty, Eloise pushes the bell that calls the residents to come for snack. Tray in hand, I push backward through the swinging doors. It is a surprise to see that all the seats are already full, as though people have been sitting and waiting for snack all morning. I hand out the bowls of yogurt and pineapple. If Edna were here, I think, she would be sniffing at the modest portions. Eloise had measured out the yogurt using a half cup measure, and indicated that I should give only one ring of pineapple to each bowl.

Eloise motions for me to sit at a table where there are two women in wheelchairs, while she takes her place at the next one where a white-haired man in a plaid shirt sits with an old woman in a sack of a dress. I muster a smile for the women at my table, and hold out my hand to one of them.

"Hi," I say. "My name is Joan." The women blink at me, and the one with the Parkinson's-like tremors clears her throat, a sound that rattles from deep inside her

It is as if the women are waiting for me to spoon-feed them. Eloise waves a spoon at me and nods her head. That's exactly what they are waiting for, I gather.

I manoeuvre a spoon toward the lips of the first woman, whose head shakes constantly as though she is saying "no." Half the yogurt goes into her mouth, the other half smears across her lips. I don't dare try the pineapple. The other woman, looking well-fed and prim in pearl earrings, opens her mouth and waits. I spoon in yogurt and a piece of pineapple, and she gums it like a baby, a trail of yogurt making its way down her chin.

After about five minutes, a pair of personal care workers come to take the women away.

"Let's go, Mrs. Oliver. You too, Mrs. Johnson." They glance at me with some curiosity, but they don't greet me. I feel invisible and shaky. Edna had lived here, like this, for three years.

After Eloise and I take the bowls into the kitchen and wipe the tables, Eloise leads me back to the utility closet. There are buckets and mops, various cleaning fluids. Eloise shows me what to take and proceeds to the washrooms where we place "do not enter" signs in the doorways. Eloise shows me a paper on the wall where all the tasks we are to do are listed, ready to be checked off as they are completed.

To my relief, I have the women's washroom. I look at myself in the mirror. My face is pale and I can tell that my hair will stick out in all directions when I take off my hairnet. Oh Edna, how did I not see how things are? I put on a pair of industrial rubber gloves, and get ready to scrub the toilets.

Eloise finishes much before me, and comes in to inspect my work. I am struggling a bit with the bucket, and haven't started mopping the floor.

"*Non*," says Eloise, and motions for me to give her the mop. With a practiced movement, she swishes the mop back and forth as effortlessly as though she is dancing. In fact, she is dancing! And singing too. I stand and watch her, Ginger to her Fred Astaire mop. Edna would have liked her, I think.

Lunch comes and goes, with more spoon-feeding of peas and applesauce. The afternoon we spend peeling boiled eggs. I think it is a strange snack, considering how many of the residents can't feed themselves. But watching Eloise and the personal care workers, who mash the eggs in a bowl with a fork, I see that it is possible to turn almost anything into mush. Had Edna eaten this way? She had dentures of course, but something tells me that might not have been taken into consideration.

By the end of the afternoon, I am tired, but there is still the floor to mop. Eloise seems to move at exactly the same speed as she had in the morning, tirelessly swinging the mop back and forth as she sings a garbled tune. Halfway through she stops and turns to me with a small bow, handing off the mop to me. Then she puts her bomber jacket on, and takes off her hairnet. Her hair springs out in all directions, a mass of frizz, which she tucks under a large cap. I try to mop the way she had—with effortless efficiency—but I am red-faced and puffing at the end.

Eloise puts her hand on my shoulder. "Good-bye," she says. I am ready to crumble. "I go now to English school."

I shake her hand. "Goodnight. See you in the morning," I say. She smiles, her tiny face crinkling.

"Goodnight. Sleep tight. Don't let bug beds bite."

I go to see Dr. Bard that evening. I am calmly sucking on a cough drop when he ushers me into his office, to perch on the edge of the orange couch. His eyes look pained.

"I am so sorry to hear about the death of your friend," says Dr. Bard. How does he know, I wonder silently. Am I that transparent?

"Your mother called," he says. "She is especially concerned about you since Edna passed away." I should have guessed. My mother can't leave anything alone.

"I'm fine," I say.

Sitting at his desk, Dr. Bard leans back in his chair. "I can't help but notice you're having a cough drop," he says. "You were making good progress, but it seems that Edna's death has set you back a bit." He smiles, gently.

I shrug my shoulders. "It doesn't matter." I say.

"What doesn't matter?" he asks, seeming genuinely curious. I shrug again. I feel tired. Dr. Bard says, "Joan you're using the cough drops to numb out. It's a normal thing to want to stop feeling pain. Just remember why you're doing it," he says. I look up at Dr. Bard, who seems far away across his wooden desk. He is trying to throw me a life preserver, but I am already becoming a creature that belongs to the sea.

When I get home that evening my parents are talking at the kitchen table. They stop when I walk in the door, and look up at me with innocent eyes. I drop my bag on the floor and go to the counter to pour some tea, then sit down with them.

"Well?" I ask. "What's up?" They look at one another, then away.

"How was your first day of work?" my mother asks. She looked timid.

"It was fine." I say. "Eloise showed me how to mop." My father's eyebrows knit together. "There actually is a science to it," I say defensively.

"Of course there is," my mother says, soothingly.

Thirty-five

Edna's visitation is tonight. I don't stop to think who arranged it, I just go, on foot, ahead of my mother who is getting her hair done this evening. She looks at me with concern as I get ready to leave the house. I am wearing black jeans and a black turtleneck, which I figure is funereal enough.

"Wouldn't you like to get your hair done before the visitation, sweetie?" my mother asks. I wouldn't. She looks hurt, but mostly concerned and that makes me feel more miserable than if she'd just let me wallow in guilt.

I walk in the direction of the bus stop, past the Jamiesons' old house. Mrs. Jamieson died a few years ago and the house was sold to a young couple with a baby. It looks shrunken and faded—but then so do many of the houses on our street, bungalows from the '50s and '60s. Even though everything is neat and tidy and new coats of paint are meant to liven things up, it is clearly a subdivision past its heyday.

On the bus there is a group of rowdy teenagers sitting near the back, talking into their cell phones, squealing with laughter. It reminds me of how I'd never really been one—I'd somehow gone missing from my teen years, and I can't remember much about them except the dazed boredom, misery and disappointment. A longing comes over me, to be young and raucous, arms open to the future. I look at my reflection in the window across the aisle, my face pale and unsmiling. Underwater. Ghoulish.

I get off the bus at the funeral home and I hear the kids at the back of the bus call out to me, "Hey, who died?" I don't answer them. Edna died, of course.

The front hall of the funeral room is dimly lit, with candles, and there are artificial flowers standing in bowls around the room, on the fake fireplace mantel, and the side tables. A woman dressed in a pink skirt and blazer with a string of pink-tinted pearls welcomes me into the back room. I see the coffin in the dim light, and feel my heart lurch.

There are people sitting on either side of the room, in the dark. I don't think I know any of Edna's friends, but someone greets me. It's Justine. She smiles briefly at me, then turns her attention back to a man in a dark suit, who I think might be her husband. He is balding, with a paunch, and his eyes are dark and small. Like Edna's. He speaks with a thick accent, struggling for the English words—but there is something bland and detached about him. He is speaking, to everyone, to no one in particular, looking off into the atmosphere.

"My mother tell me she has good life in Canada. Don't worry, Tibor, she tell me. You take care your father. He has heart problem. He need help every day." Tibor sighs softly, a sound like doves cooing, a self-comforting sound. "My father tell me she is dead, many, many years ago. Then she call me. She is crying." He looks down at his meaty hands, palms up, in his lap. I sit there, stunned. Edna has a son?

Tibor continues. "You take care your business, she say. I am fine...She tell me she marry a doctor, but he die...I don't know she is sick—that she live in hospital." He puts his head in his hands. It is hard to say whether he is grieving or thinking.

Justine puts her arm around him. "There, there, it's alright," she says and puts out her hand to me as though to gather me in, to link me to this man. "Tibor, this is Joan. She was a friend of your mother's."

Tibor looks up at me. "She took care of me when I was a child," I stammer. "She was my favourite person." It's true.

Tibor gazes at me, then leans his mouth against his fist. His eyes are like Edna's but there is something different about them—her ferocity is wholly missing from him. It is hard to know what he is thinking.

Someone with a raspy voice pipes up. "Why don't we sing?" I am not sure if that is what is done at visitations. Someone begins "Amazing Grace" and a few voices pitch in from the dark.

Tibor looks up. His face is streaked with tears that glow in the candlelight, and he seems to be mouthing the words to some other song, or perhaps the same song, in Hungarian. I see his mouth make a small "o" and then he closes his eyes, and rocks slightly, back and forth, crossing himself several times. Justine keeps one hand on his shoulder, at the same time wiping a tear from his cheek. It may be a practiced efficiency, but for some reason, it is comforting.

I get up quietly and go to the half-opened casket, at the dark and almost neglected end of the visitation room. Edna lies there with her curly hair framing her face, held in perfect place by a dose of hairspray. She is tastefully powdered and rouged, and looks ten years younger, in a flower-print dress. I can't help but think of a doll in plastic packaging, its eyes closed until it is made to stand up, and the long, lashed lids pop open. I almost expect her to grab me by the arm and tell me it's too dark and I should put the light on or I will strain my eyes. Her hands, which never rested while she lived, are clasped peacefully on her breast, holding a white flower—not a rose or a lily, but a carnation. As the others sing, I open my purse, furtively, and take out a square of knitting, about the size of the bottom of a milk carton, which I tuck under Edna's arm. Then I kiss her cheek and go back to sit down, knowing that I have finally accomplished something.

As we are filing out of the funeral parlour, Tibor stands at the door to shake everyone's hands. When it is my turn, he grasps my hand in both of his and shakes it.

"You my sister," he says. I am taken aback. "My mother care for you like...daughter. You visit her every week." So Edna had told him about me—but she had never told me about him.

"You come to Hungary to visit me, yes?" I move my head in a non-committal way, half shake, half nod. Then he smiles, his eyes slightly unfocussed, and lets go of my hand. None of Edna's blazing kindness. But she was there, lurking in the corners of his mouth.

When I get home my mother is sitting in the kitchen, reading the paper, looking newly-minted with her perfect hair. She has painted her nails, a dark red, almost bloody, and is waving them in the air, like a musical conductor, in slow motion. When she hears me come in she looks up quickly.

"Oh Joan, I missed the visitation. My hair appointment went overtime," she says with what sounds like true regret. I sit down opposite her, but don't look at her.

"Edna's son was there," I say, grabbing the classifieds. Job ads. Short order cook. Part-time cleaner. Bank manager. It doesn't hurt to look, even though I have a job.

My mother puts the paper down.

"Edna's son?" She spreads out her hands on the table, like a peacock fan. Were they still drying? "What's he like?" she asks. I look up at her. Her nose wrinkles slightly. Nervously.

"You knew she had a son?" I ask.

She smiles at me quickly, then sighs. "Joan, Edna didn't want to tell you. When you were little, she thought it would just be too confusing for you—why she left her young son back in Hungary and came to Canada. She thought you would misunderstand. And since she never told you, it was easier just to go on not telling you."

I stare at her. "What's to misunderstand?" I ask.

My mother looks down. And then she says, "Why would any mother leave her child to come to a foreign country, and never see him again?"

I think about a young Edna, a buxom, curly haired young woman, pulling a young boy after her by the hand down a narrow cobblestone street. He strains in the other direction, after a horse cart, a flower monger, a soldier in uniform. Edna keeps yanking him back, but suddenly, he breaks free and is gone around the corner. She stands there, hands open. Then closes them. Then keeps on walking.

My mother looks up at me. She is thinking something complicated—her eyes see me, but also something else. "Why would she do that?" she asks again, more to herself this time than to me.

Then my mother tells me the tale—the secret story of Edna's life before she came to Canada more than half a century ago. Edna was a teenager, living with her widowed mother when she met Tibor's father, Josef, who was in his early twenties, and handsome, with black hair and high cheekbones under his tan skin. Josef's father had a small farm, but also a grocery stand in Budapest which Josef worked. Edna would buy radishes and peppers from him for her own mother, and he would tease her, saying she must like things hot and spicy. Edna retorted that he'd never find out for himself, thank you very much. His dark eyes narrowed. Now she was a challenge.

One Saturday when he was closing his grocery stall, he gave her a strange vegetable that she had never seen before. It was a yellow summer squash shaped, she thought, like a flying saucer. She thanked him and took it. He invited her to a pub for a drink. Edna declined. He ran his hand through his hair. Well then, would she like to go to the cinema?

Edna loved movies. Though her mother was waiting for her

to bring home vegetables for supper, she accepted. Edna took her summer squash under one arm and walked with Josef into her future.

At the movie theatre, they sat in the back row. Josef was amorous and Edna, who felt his hand on her breast, awakened to a whole world inside her that she had not previously been aware of. She bit his ear so hard that he yelped.

When she arrived home, still holding on to the summer squash, her mother took one look at her, flushed and dewy as a rose, and slapped her face. Edna went to bed without supper, her hand over the mark of her mother's hand on her cheek.

They spent many a hot summer evening in the back of the movie theatre. Fall was a busy time for Josef, and Edna stayed with him till dark, helping him pack up what was left of his produce. Then one fall evening, Josef invited her to visit him on his father's farm for a weekend. She could stay the night, he said, in his sisters' room. He wouldn't try anything. His eyes were so black and penetrating, they were like wells. She looked into them and could see herself, reflected back. She agreed, without even thinking about what her mother would say.

But as she walked home, she composed a lie for her mother. I will tell her I am going to pick berries with Katusha, she thought. I am going to take care of Katusha's little sister while her family goes to visit their relatives. I am going...Nothing sounded quite right. Her mother would know she was lying— she always did.

Edna walked in the front door. "Mama, Josef has invited me to his father's farm this weekend," she said.

Her mama held her face between her hands. "Little one, that is a good sign. That means Josef has a mind to marry you."

Edna was so shocked that she bit down on her tongue and it began to bleed.

The next weekend, Edna went with Josef on his horse cart to

his father's farm, ten miles outside the city. She had never been to a farm before and didn't know what to expect. The house was low and sprawling under a red tiled roof, surrounded by a vegetable patch that was clearly in its end-of-summer straggly stage. There were chickens inside a fenced off yard and ducks, a few fruit trees. Although it was clearly a place of work, Edna felt there was something forlorn and neglected looking about it.

Josef must have been conscious of the impression his home made on her, because he quickly ushered her inside to where his mother was surrounded by buckets of grapes.

"We're making wine tomorrow," his mother told Edna, smiling as she extended her worn hand. Edna took it. It felt warm and rough. Josef's father looked up at her from the horse tack he was mending, and grunted a greeting. Josef's two younger sisters peered curiously at her from the back door to the kitchen garden where they were digging potatoes.

That night they ate and drank a great deal. Josef's father, red-faced, sang Hungarian folk songs in a loud and slightly off-key tenor, and the rest of the family laughed as he stood and swayed in front of the fire. Josef slapped him on the back. His father, pleased and embarrassed sat down and promptly went to sleep. Josef's mother and sisters began to tidy the room of mugs and bottles, and Josef took Edna outside to look at the stars.

The air was frosty. Josef held her against the back of the house and pushed himself against her. She looked up at the stars, their tiny, brilliant sparks against the cold wall of sky. Josef's warm tongue softly mined her teeth, her gums and throat.

"I love you Orsolia," he said as he strained against her. Then suddenly he groaned and grew limp, a dark damp spot on the front of his trousers. Edna, her panties around her ankles, felt a chill of disappointment. Josef tried to laugh.

"It's better to wait until we are married," he said, to hide his shame. Edna put her arms around him and kissed his stubbly cheek.

"It doesn't matter," she crooned, "all will be well."

Edna went to bed in the room of Josef's sisters, who were already breathing softly and rhythmically—as though they were on horseback, running on the beach. Outside the window, the stars slowly turned. Edna's eyes closed and in her dream, frost crept across the window. Ferns unfurling, crystal parapets, threads of glass.

She was awakened by a hand over her mouth, the sour smell of alcohol. Josef's father. He undid his trousers with the other hand and opened her legs roughly. She turned her head and saw his girls, asleep. She lay as still as possible under Josef's father, listening to his heavy breathing and the whispered vulgarities and endearments, his rhythmic grunting. It hurt but she didn't cry out. She kept her eyes on Josef's sisters, their brows as smooth and pale as the moon. They stood on the shore of childhood, innocent as deer.

When he finally rolled off her, she sat up in the bed. He looked up at her with half-closed eyes, bleary with drink.

"I'm sorry," he slurred, "I'm sorry." She took his arm and pushed him up and away from her.

"Go, before your daughters awaken," she told him. He stumbled out of the room, listing like a ship on a stormy sea.

Edna lay in bed, staring at the ceiling. She could feel something inside her. A bud, a seed rooting.

The next morning there was blood on the sheets.

"It is my time of the month," she apologized to Josef's mother, who smiled at her and put her hand on Edna's shoulder.

"Never mind," she said. Edna sat at the breakfast table with Josef, who gazed at her longingly as he spooned porridge into his mouth. She couldn't eat anything.

"I am not feeling well," she said. Josef's face fell.

His mother looked at her kindly. "Josef will drive you back into town today, with his last load of vegetables of the season," she said.

Josef's father was still asleep when they set off. Josef gave Edna a pair of his work gloves to protect her hands from the cold. He talked about his need for her, but she felt far away, a spot on the horizon. They passed a wooded lot, where the brown leaves of the oak still clung to its branches and rattled in the wind.

"Stop here," she said and she went into the woods to relieve herself. The stinging brought tears to her eyes.

A little way off, Josef stood with his back to her, a stream of warm piss falling to the ground. She watched him for a moment, then, before he had a chance to fasten his trousers, she went to him. When he felt her hand on his arm he turned and pulled her to him and pushed her down into the leaves. For the second time she felt the weight of a man, and endured it. She gazed up at him detached, his face contorted with intense effort. Until finally he slumped against her shoulder and cried, kissing her face covered with his own tears.

When the baby was born, he would think it was his child, she told herself. She felt a terrible fluttering emptiness for this deception. It was as if the very pointed end of a wedge had been driven between them and was prying them from one another.

Josef drove Edna home. In a month she would tell him she was pregnant. He lifted her off the cart. He would marry her and no one would know the difference. He kissed her gently on the mouth. She grew cold, knowing she would have to move to Josef's father's farm. He waved over his shoulder to her as he drove away. She stood in front of her mother's door, her arm raised in farewell.

Edna turned to go into her mother's house. Her mother stood in the doorway. Edna knew that her mother knew, somehow.

"Ma, Josef's father did this to me," she said. Her mother raised a handkerchief to her lips. Edna felt like crying, curled up in a ball in her mother's arms. But she said, "I will marry Josef and live on his father's farm. But I will not stay."

Edna's mother looked at her with tenderness and pity. "My daughter," she said. "I understand. I will help you. You will go to Canada."

Thirty-six

The next morning I lie in bed staring at the ceiling. Edna's story—what does it mean? It means that Edna, who had been in my life for thirty years, was not the person I thought she was. It means she had hidden herself from me like a clam, buried in the sand. But she had told my mother. How was it that after all these years, Edna could keep such a secret from me?

I realize I have taken a cough drop from my side table without even knowing it. It sits under my tongue, melting into sweet and bitter. *Edna, why?* There is a conflagration in my mind and a rumbling in my chest. *What is it?* My face grows hot. Anger like a volcanic eruption pours out of me as tears. I turn over and put my face in my pillow so my parents won't hear my sobbing.

It is seven-thirty and I am to be at work for eight. I don't shower or eat breakfast. When I have finished crying I go to the bathroom and see my face in the mirror, blotchy and red. *Edna, you don't even know what you've done to me.* I wash the angry red away with cold water.

I forgive you, Edna. I forgive you. I repeat those words many times as I dress myself for work. But each time I think about what she's done, anger wells up inside me again.

Eloise is spooning applesauce into bowls when I arrive. She smiles at me, but all I can do in return is to blow my nose. My head feels stuffy from crying. Eloise's eyebrows knit together— she looks worried.

"It's okay," I tell her. "It's nothing." I look at the snack schedule. It says apple juice and pudding. I beckon to Eloise. "Snack today—not apple sauce—apple juice." Eloise puts the palm of her hand to her forehead. I start dumping the contents of the bowls back into the tub of apple sauce.

"It's okay Eloise," I say. Her eyes look pained, as though she is grieving.

Eloise grabs my elbow. "Your friend—Edna," she says. I step back. How does she know? "Justine tell me," she says, looking down. I nod.

"It's okay," I say, "I'm okay," and for that moment, I mean it.

I take a tub of pistachio pudding out of the fridge. Edna's favourite. Eloise watches me. "Pudding," I say. "Pudding is sweet. There are different kinds—vanilla, butterscotch, chocolate..."

Eloise's eyes open wide. "Mmm, *chocolat*."

"This one is green," I say. "It is made from pistachio nuts." Eloise looks confused. "Pistachio?" I ask. "Do you know pistachio?" She nods, then shakes her head.

Where did she come from, I wonder. Somewhere there aren't any pistachio nuts? I decide I'll bring her some next time. "Where do you come from?" I ask. Eloise nods her head. I try again. "What country do you come from?"

Eloise brightens. "I come from the Democratic Republic of Congo," she says, as though reading from a textbook. Africa, I think. Eloise continues, "We have war there." She shakes her head. "Many people die." She smiles and shakes her head again. "My mother, father, all gone."

I don't know why she is smiling. "Eloise," I say. "I am sorry." I wonder whether my feelings about Edna's death are any match for hers.

Eloise puts her hand on mine. "No," she says. I take it to mean I shouldn't compare griefs with her. "No," she says again, smiling. "Sad. Both." She doesn't look sad, I think. But maybe it is just too big a sadness to show on one woman's face.

Thirty-seven

I work all day and I am tired. So tired. All I want to do is go home, put my pyjamas on, disappear. But instead I shower and put on my best dress, which I haven't worn since last year. It is tight but I don't care. Edna deserves it.

I worry Tibor will grab my hand again and call me his sister. But I have to go to the wake. It is the last time I can see Edna.

Tibor is bleary, his eyes red with grief. I don't think he recognizes anyone. I sit in the back row with my mother, who made us late because she was fussing over the sympathy card. When we get to the funeral home, someone is already giving a eulogy. It isn't anyone I recognize. I see the back of Justine's head in the front row, next to Tibor, who is sobbing quietly.

The person giving the eulogy, I figure out, is someone from her church. A woman who has known her for maybe ten years. She speaks about Edna's kindness, her compassion for people in need, her firm faith. To me it doesn't really sound like Edna, at least not the whole of Edna. Nowhere does she mention Edna's magic in the kitchen, baking and cooking and ironing. Or Edna's sweet voice, or her ferocious loyalty. And she doesn't mention that Edna had been raped, that Mrs. Jamieson had kicked her out, and that she'd been secretly in love with Dr. Jamieson. And she doesn't mention that Edna, though addled at the end, had enough presence of mind and generosity of spirit to protect her son from the truth, that he is really his father's brother.

Tibor stands up and wipes his eyes with a handkerchief on the way to the podium. He is almost an old man, I think. He is actually old enough to be my father. Tibor begins to babble something, which sounds half Hungarian, half English. He waves his handkerchief in the air. Justine comes to his side and speaks into his ear.

"Yes! Yes!" he says, as though struck by a bolt of lightning. "Yes! If anyone would like to say something, about my mother, I would be so happy."

Justine stares over the heads of the guests, at me. I stand up. My mother looks surprised. Tibor beckons with both hands.

"Here is Joan," he says. "My mother take care of her when she is child." He hugs my shoulders, and steps back from the microphone.

I look out over the sea of faces. Most have white hair, or no hair—they must be the older members of Edna's church. And then with a shock I recognize Ricky, Edna's old paperboy. He is my age, but he looks much the same as when he was a teenager, just a little thicker around the jaw.

My mind is a jumble. I want to say something that will let people know who Edna was, but it is hard to know how to start.

"Edna." I say. And stop. Justine squeezes my hand. "One time Edna made a dress for me. When I was little. It was blue with bunches of cherries all over it. I loved that dress." I say. The audience is quiet. "She taught me to knit this year. I'm making a scarf."

That is almost all I have to say. "Edna has beautiful handwriting," I conclude. Tibor looks at me kindly, and thanks me. Justine smiles.

I go back to sit next to my mother. Her forehead is slightly wrinkled, as though she is worried or perplexed—but she smiles at me. I sit down and, as if I have just been relieved of a heavy weight that I've been carrying on my shoulders, I feel them float up toward my ears, aching.

There is singing. It is a few members of the choir from Edna's church, dressed in black robes. They sway slightly, singing a few other hymns I don't recognize. The audience joins in, and then there are prayers led by the Catholic priest, Father Daniel. He looks tired and slightly rumpled, as though he's just got up from a nap. I wonder if Edna ever made him her poppy seed cake, and if she kept her bottle of gin under his sink at the rectory when she worked for him.

There is a reception afterward. Ladies from the church are putting sandwiches and sweets on plates, and bustling around the kitchen, making coffee and tea. I stand with my mother off to one side, planning to drink a cup of coffee and then leave. Ricky is standing by himself in another corner. He's looking at me, though I don't think he could possibly recognize me. I turn slightly away from him, toward—no one. My mother has wandered a few feet away to speak with Tibor. I can tell she is having trouble understanding his accent, because she keeps pushing her hair behind her ear and tipping her head toward him.

Just as I am becoming convinced that Ricky Hauser does indeed recognize me, Justine comes over, pushing Mrs. Oliver in her wheelchair.

"Wasn't that a lovely service?" she asks. "I am sure Edna would have liked it." I want to say I think Edna would have liked a little more colour, maybe. A bottle of gin and some wailing. Mrs. Oliver clears her throat, but says nothing.

"Hi Joan," someone says beside me. It is Ricky. Somehow he has made his way across the crowded room to where I am. He looks older, now that I can see him up close, and he's wearing a black sports jacket, along with a white shirt and black jeans.

I look at his feet, at his black sneakers, and then at his face. He must know I am shocked to see him. "Do you remember me? Ricky Hauser. We were in math class together."

He sat in the back of the class with the jokers. Never a troublemaker himself, always polite, pleasant and attentive—that's how a teacher would describe him. But if they asked him a question, he would smile, and shake his head. I'm sorry, I don't know the answer, he would say. The teacher would sigh, and the jokers would snicker, but Ricky would go on smiling apologetically, listening to the teacher explain quadratic equations again, and not understanding. It was as though he were some cheerful being from another planet, to whom math class was an enjoyable but incomprehensible experience. He was just along for the ride, not caring where he'd end up.

"You were Edna's paperboy," I say. Then correct myself. "The Jamiesons' paperboy." Somehow he had never delivered the paper to our house—some little kid brought it early in the morning.

Ricky looks pleased and surprised. "That's right," he says. "But it was Edna I dealt with." I imagine him coming to the door with the paper and Edna passing him a homemade cookie and a tip at Christmas. "Edna and I went to the same church." You used to smoke pot at the back of the school at lunch hour, I think to myself.

"What are you up to these days?" he asks. I look down at my feet.

"I'm working in the nursing home Edna lived in," I say. He nods and smiles. "You?" I ask.

"Well I'm, um, self-employed," he says. "I paint fences, clean garages, do a little gardening. For seniors mostly. Shut-ins."

For some reason, that all makes sense to me. From pot-smoking paperboy to serf for seniors. I can see him in old jeans and work gloves, working away, chatting amiably to little old ladies when they totter over to inspect his weeding. Flashing them his untroubled smile. Lighting up a spliff when they are out of range.

"I guess we're in the same line of work then," I say grudgingly, although I try not to show it. But I don't have to worry. Ricky's face lights up, as if I have made a brilliant observation.

"Yes I guess you could say that!" he agrees. "I like working with old people," he says. "They're so...kind. Edna meant a lot to me."

I feel my face heat up. I don't know what to say to that, so I glance over at my mother.

She is backing away, apologetically, from Tibor who is waving his hands in the air, his balding pate a bright pink.

"I guess I should go," I tell Ricky, taking a sideways step toward my mother. He shakes my hand.

"It was really nice to see you," he says. "Maybe we could go for coffee sometime?" He has caught me off guard, but I shrug noncommittally.

"Sure," I say. "See you around."

My mother smiles quickly, a glint of panic in her eyes and stretches out her arm toward me. Tibor grabs my other hand and pumps it warmly.

"Joan," he says, expelling a breath of heat and alcohol, his eyes blurry. "I tell your mother—you come to Hungary to work for me. You need good job, I need English. You help me?" he asks. I shrug again. I feel Ricky's eyes watching me.

"Um, sorry Tibor, but I want to stay in Nova Scotia," I say. "I have a boyfriend here." I can feel a shock wave run though my mother. Tibor clasps my hand in both of his.

"Is good. When you marry, you bring husband to work for me." He leans toward me, and tries to wink, but both his eyelids flutter. "And you bring your mother." He gazes down at her, and her cheeks flush.

I turn to see Ricky's back as he makes his way through the crowd of people. He seems to kind of melt in and out, like a liquid, never bumping anyone, never having to say excuse me.

I feel a pang of...I don't know what. His cheerfulness mystifies me—it is like some valuable substance, saffron, bright and inexplicable.

My mother and I step out into the dark air. There is frost on the ground already, and we crunch over the grass to the car. Warmth wafts off my mother—the heat of embarrassment.

"Do you really have a boyfriend?" she asks as she fiddles with the front door lock. For the first time in a long time, I laugh. I feel strangely peaceful, as though something has been laid to rest. Edna is sleeping in the funeral parlour, and it is time to go home. Tomorrow my life will begin again. It is as though I have been stalled in a car at the traffic lights, and have only just managed to get the engine to turn over. I hope Edna will forgive me, but I am going to keep driving until I can't go any further, until I leave the city limits of this life.

Thirty-eight

Eloise is off sick. I picture her thin frame bent over the toilet, throwing up. A flu is going around Mount Pleasant, and a lot of the older people have had it. Justine comes into the kitchen before snack time and says she has a replacement worker for the day. Ricky Hauser is standing behind her. My mouth hangs open. How is this possible?

Ricky smiles at me, an easy, untroubled smile. Justine says, "Can you show Ricky where to find a hairnet? You're the top dog here today," nodding in my direction. I feel as though the sky has caved in.

Ricky follows me down the hall to the utility closet. "I didn't think I'd be seeing you so soon," he says. "Justine hired me last night as backup." Justine hired Ricky at Edna's wake? It's too much. I nod, fuming. If I'd known when I was hired that Ricky Hauser would be working here, I probably would have thought twice about taking the job. "Edna meant a lot to me," he'd said. What right does he have to Edna at all?

Ricky puts the hairnet on. With his hair off his face he has an almost bovine docility, I think. What affection could Edna have had for such a person? But there is something, a spark of intelligence in his eyes that I haven't ever noticed before.

"There are the washrooms to clean," I say briskly. "Morning and afternoon snack. We serve lunch, although it's cooked off premises. Then there's whatever cleaning needs doing in the lunch room."

Ricky nods. "Where would you like me to start?"

I think about the washrooms. Can I give him both? No, I sigh. I better go by the book. "Snack's up next. It's graham crackers and cream cheese."

Ricky and I stand at the counter, spreading cheese on crackers.

"You know," he says, turning to me. "I'm really glad to get the chance to work with you. I know Edna would be happy that we finally met up again." My face reddens. What did he know about what would make Edna happy?

"I know we were on different pages in high school," he says meekly. "But I guess now we have Edna in common." My knife clatters to the floor.

"Excuse me," I say, coughing and rushing out of the kitchen. A personal care worker pulls a woman walking with a walker toward her, out of my way. I end up at the women's washroom, splashing water on my face for the second time in two days. Ricky Hauser is as dense as a block of cheese, if he doesn't know I despise him. I suck hard on a cough drop, but it doesn't seem to make a difference.

When I finally collect myself, it is snack time. Ricky has carried the trays out to the tables himself, and is chatting with the old woman at Eloise's table. She nods wisely, as if he is telling her something worth hearing. I plunk myself down with Mrs. Johnson and Mrs. Oliver, who seem oblivious to the fact that no one is feeding them.

Ricky speaks across the table to me. "You alright?" he asks, concerned. I nod. Mrs. Oliver's head shakes "no." I get busy feeding her and Mrs. Johnson so I won't have to talk to Ricky Hauser.

That afternoon, I give Ricky washroom duty after all, so I can be alone in the kitchen. It is quiet except for the fridge humming, and the muffled sounds from the hallway. I open the door to the backyard, and stand in the doorway. This is a time someone who smoked would light up a cigarette, so I allow myself a cough drop and suck peacefully. It is sunny and cool, the time of year I love more than any other. If only Edna were here. Into my mind, unbidden, comes an image of Edna, conducting a group of musicians in tails, and Ricky Hauser, with Eloise in his arms, gliding across the kitchen floor. It angers me that even in my daydreams, I can't stop Ricky Hauser from making an appearance.

That night, despite my parents' wanting to take me out for supper, I go to bed early. When I refuse such an offer they know something is really wrong. They hover in the kitchen as I eat leftover chilli and their worried eyes follow me on my way to bed. I hear them talking together in a whisper and I take comfort in the fact that they seem closer than ever lately, even if it is due to the worry I cause them.

It occurs to me, as I lay there, that Edna *liked* Ricky. She must have, if she let him visit her. And that she had never told me, just as she had never mentioned her son, Tibor. Why did she have so many secrets, I wonder. As the flower of darkness unfurls around me, the pain of everything she hadn't told me beats inside me like a heart.

Eloise is back to work the next day. She has a cough that rattles through her like a freight train. "I must work," she says, when I ask her why she isn't home in bed. "No time for sickness." After a few attempts, she makes me understand that she has a son, and that she needs her sick days to care for him when he is sick.

Eloise seems too frail and young to have a son. Her face barely looks twenty, and physically, she resembles a girl of thirteen. She takes a photo from her wallet to show me. Her son is about five years old, a beautiful brown child with the eyes of his mother. She gazes at him adoringly.

"He know good English," she says, and puts her fist to her mouth to stifle a cough.

Edna would cook her some chicken soup, I think. But I can distract her with an English lesson.

"He knows how to speak English well, does he?"

Eloise nods.

"We can practice English," I say. Her eyebrows shoot up.

"Yes, yes, practice!" she says.

"Eloise, I'm going to pour the juice. Do you know the word *pour*?"

"Yes, yes," she says excitedly. "Poor. Not much money."

I put my hand on her arm. "No," I say. "*Pour*, like to *pour* juice. Now I am *pouring* juice into a cup," I demonstrate. I write the word on the clipboard hanging over the counter. Her forehead wrinkles.

"Pour?" she says. "*En francais*, *pour*. Same as English *for*," she says. She shakes her head to one side, as though she has water in her ear.

I decide to try a nursery rhyme. "Listen, Eloise. This is a children's song. I'm a little teapot, short and stout. Here is my handle, here is my spout." I do the motions awkwardly and point to a teapot on the shelf above us. Eloise watches with rapt attention. "When I get all steamed up, hear me shout, Just tip me over and pour me out!"

Eloise is charmed. "*Encore*," she says. I look over my shoulder at the kitchen door.

"Okay once more," I say. But in the middle of "I'm a Little Teapot," Justine enters the kitchen, and Eloise turns quickly and busies herself at the counter.

"It's past time for afternoon snack to be on the table," she says disapprovingly, hand on hip. "The residents are waiting. What are you doing, Joan?" she asks cocking her head to look at me.

"I'm a little teapot," I say sheepishly. Eloise covers her mouth and giggles. Justine gazes at me in disbelief.

"It's canned pears today," I tell Eloise, pointing to a large can that needs opening. "I will *pour* the milk," I tell her.

Justine's face darkens. "Keep your English lessons focused on the job," she says, turning on one small heel and disappearing through the double doors. Eloise laughs soundlessly behind her hand.

Over the next few days, I teach Eloise a number of nursery rhymes, including "Little Miss Muffet" and "Hey Diddle Diddle." She says them to herself as she prepares snack or loads the dishwasher, and while mopping. I am surprised how quickly she picks them up, as though she is hungry and they are bread. I also teach her Raffi songs, which she loves. And on Friday I give her a picture book with the words of the song "Baby Beluga" that I bought during a short stint working in a daycare. Eloise looks wild from trying not to cry.

The next Monday she brings me a coconut pie. "Good, *delicieuse*, you eat," she says. I try a spoonful. It is better than my mother's favourite coconut squares, which always seem funereal, since she served some to me while the ambulance took Mr. Tulley's body away. Eyes open wide, I nod my thanks. Eloise chortles and hides the pie in the refrigerator before Justine can see it.

Eloise and I talk about many things. She tells me about her other job in a bakery, the things her son is learning at school, about her English classes. We talk a little about Edna, whom Eloise remembered only from the ambulance coming to take her corpse away. I like to talk to Eloise about Edna, whose prowess in the kitchen and facility with knitting needles Eloise can appreciate. But I can tell Eloise is waiting for something more. Every time I come up against the story of why Edna left Hungary, I feel my face redden and my throat go dry. I still felt betrayed, and confounded, by her decades-long silence about the fact she had a son and by her friendship with Ricky Hauser.

Eloise watches my face. She can see there is something I haven't told her.

One day I come to work and Ricky is there, peeling bananas for snack. Eloise is standing beside him, her arm in a cast.

"What happened?" I ask her, ignoring Ricky. He turns toward me, smiling. His face looks new, fresh as a baby.

Eloise looks down. "I fall," she says, her eyes skittering across the floor. "All fall down," she says, smiling. "I come for English lesson!"

I look at the kitchen door. What would Justine think?

"Eloise—how about this?" I usher her toward the door. "We can meet after work. For half an hour in the coffee shop at the hospital. Justine will be angry if she sees you here when I'm working."

Eloise nods. "Yes, yes," she says, "okay." She waves at Ricky. "Bye bye, Rick-ee!"

He raises an arm toward her, holding a banana peel.

It occurs to me that if Eloise's arm is broken, Ricky might be working with me for the next six weeks or more. I feel queasy.

Ricky starts slicing the bananas into rounds. I arrange some bowls on a tray and get the yogurt out of the fridge. Ricky smiles brightly at me.

"How long are you here for?" I ask.

Ricky shrugs. "It all depends on when Eloise can come back," he says. "She broke her arm pretty badly, in a couple places."

I picture Eloise on skates, thin legs flailing. "How did it happen?"

Ricky shrugs. "Eloise tried to tell me," he says. "We had a hard time understanding each other." Ricky's face reddens. "My French was never very good."

I look at him. Is he...embarrassed? "I never was that good in school," he says, "Not like you." He smiles. I feel my own face flush.

It occurs to me that Ricky has changed. He is no longer completely without self-consciousness, or oblivious to the requirements of this world. He actually feels embarrassed by what he sees as a shortcoming. Grudgingly, I give him a point for that. I hadn't realized I've been waiting for a reason to stop despising him.

But what did Edna see in Ricky? I wonder. During our teen years, he'd been good looking, with hair down to his shoulders, an untroubled face and priceless smile. It occurs to me that maybe Edna felt a motherly impulse toward him and for some reason, and that makes me angry. Why would she choose someone like Ricky, who was stoned out of his gourd half the time, to lavish her affection on?

Ricky's blush has subsided. He looks like his old self, peaceful and cheerful.

We carry snack out to the masses on two big trays. The residents are sitting glumly at their tables. Ricky makes a point of saying hello to each person individually, though he rarely receives a response. I think of the way Edna would see him—a nice young man, with good manners, who respects his elders. What does Edna know?

As usual, Ricky sits with Eloise's people—Mr. Carter and Mrs. Otis—and I plunk myself down with Mrs. Oliver and Mrs. Johnson. Mrs. Oliver's tremors seem worse today.

"Are you feeling okay?" I ask her. Her head shakes "no" but for the first time she speaks to me.

"Yes, dear, I'm alright," she croaks. Mrs. Johnson, dressed in a pink cardigan and pearls, smiles primly, her hands limp in her lap.

As I feed them, I think of how people I went to high school with are feeding their own babies and working responsible jobs, not gazing on the end of life, as I am. How had Edna felt to live here, among these people. Did she know her life was coming to a close, and did she miss her younger self? It pains me to think she might have weighed her present against her past and realized that her future was dwindling to mere nothingness.

Old age is treacherous, certainly. In the end, it stole from Edna her own mind. But not enough of it that she could no longer hide herself from me. It is a nail in my heart that she kept her friendship from Ricky from me and that she never shared the story of her son Tibor. Why had she hidden these things? It is as though I only knew half of Edna. The other half had been underwater, floating like an iceberg.

Ricky and I clean up the dining room in silence. I try my best not to speak to him for the rest of the day, but there is always the need to discuss who will do what. This afternoon, I say merely, "I'll do the washrooms," just to make sure there is no need to argue. Ricky looks at me, meekly, and nods.

At the end of the day, Ricky mops the kitchen floor while I unload the dishwasher. He stops mid-mop and asks, "Joan, why are you so angry?" I stop. He doesn't even know.

"I'm not angry," I say. "I'm pissed off." He looks confused, as though he is trying to understand. And then I say it. "Edna didn't tell me about Tibor. She didn't tell me about you. What else didn't she tell me about?" I slam the dishwasher closed.

Ricky looks embarrassed. "Joan. I didn't know Edna that well, but I know she thought the world of you."

I am crying, and my tears feel hot. It is the last thing I want, to cry in front of Ricky Hauser.

Ricky pats my arm. "It's okay," he says in his mild way.

"Edna wouldn't have done anything to hurt you." I know it's true. I wipe my nose on my sleeve.

"Can I give you a drive down the road to the hospital?" Ricky adds, helpfully, "Where you're meeting Eloise?"

Oh yes. Eloise. "Thanks," I say. "I'll grab my coat."

On the short drive in Ricky's truck, he tells me he had visited Edna in her last days. It is hard to hear. She had given him something, he says as the truck pulls into the hospital parking lot. Before he even stops the truck, I scramble out.

"Thanks, bye," I shout. Ricky looks deflated. "See you tomorrow," I say, gritting my teeth in a grin.

Eloise is sitting in the coffee shop when I get there. When she sees me, she smiles radiantly, and pushes forward her son to meet me, a boy with a big head and her big brown eyes. He is older than he looked in the photo she'd shown me—about eight years old, and comes up to her shoulder.

"Joan, my son, Henri," Eloise says, beaming. Henri looks at me sullenly, shrinking back toward his mother when I hold out my hand. "We practice English, I am glad," she says, pulling Henri to sit on her lap. He pushes her away and goes to sit on the floor to play with some trucks.

Eloise smiles and takes my hand. "You, here, quickly," she says, using her fingers to show me running.

I look down. "Ricky gave me a drive."

Eloise nods. "Ah Ricky," she says slyly, and laughs. "He is nice." I shake my head. I don't even want to think about it.

"I want to know one word," says Eloise, rustling through some yellow foolscap covered in notes. "It is...*ram-bunk-shus*," she says triumphantly. My eyebrows shoot up. "Nurse tell me, he is *rambunctious*," she says proudly, pointing to her son. "What means?"

I think a little. "It means full of energy, a little bit wild," I say. Eloise's forehead wrinkles. "Wild," I say, digging deep for my high school French. "*Sauvage*."

"*Ah*," Eloise nods. "Yes, *Henri est un peu sauvage*," she says, looking slightly worried. She ruffles his hair with one hand and he shrugs it off. He is making noises, like a truck backing up.

Eloise smiles at me. "So, you are well, you have good day?"

"It was okay," I murmur, surprised to think that even though Ricky was there, that yes, it was okay. "How about you?"

Eloise nods. "I go shopping. I live just there," she points to a side road across the street. "Very near."

I am not sure what to ask her. It is hardly the place to sing "I'm a Little Tea Pot." But Eloise fires a lot of questions at me.

"Where you live?" she asks.

"At home with my parents," I say, slightly embarrassed.

Her eyes open wide. "You very lucky," she says. "My father is dead, *ma mere*." Her eyes wander over to her son. "Is hard," she says. Henri is making two action figures fight one another.

I clear my throat. "I'll be moving out soon, once I find an apartment," I say. It is the first I'd given it any thought.

Eloise is immediately enthusiastic. "You come live with us!" she says, brightening.

I think for a moment. "No, Eloise, I couldn't," I say. She looks crestfallen. "I'm like a bull elephant," I tell her. She squints at me, confused. "I need my space."

"Ah," says Eloise, who smiles and shakes her head. "Canadian peoples need spaces."

"Eloise, how did you break your arm?" I ask. She frowns, looking thoughtful. Then she makes sure her son is out of range—he is sitting at a nearby table, making his action figures jump all over it.

"Joan, you don't tell anyone?" she asks. I shake my head. "Henri break my arm. He is too…rambunctious." Henri's voice is loud, as one action figure shouts at the other. "The nurse say it is an accident. Is true, but he was angry at me." She shakes her head sadly. "He need a father." I imagine Henri pulling Eloise's arm until she falls forward and it breaks.

The next day Ricky is off sick and I am on my own. It is exhausting to do all the work by myself, and by the middle of the day, I am wishing Ricky were there. His cheerful, unbothered look would be a soothing antidote to my stress, I think. There are always more cough drops, and I do use them, but they can't share the work with me.

The day after, Ricky shows up, looking pale and drawn. I muster a smile at him, and he brightens immediately.

"Sorry I was off yesterday," he says. "I spent all the night before throwing up." He shakes his head at the memory.

I am pouring juice for snack. "Don't worry," I say. "I did okay." Looking down at the juice, I realize I am blushing.

Ricky and I don't talk much, which is kind of nice, I think. We work side by side, caught up in our own thoughts. Ricky is still not completely well and sits down to rest from time to time. When he does, I can feel him looking at me as I work. Strangely, I don't feel self-conscious, but peaceful and at ease. It's a little bit like having an angel looking over my shoulder, I think with a wry smile.

Eloise and I have agreed to meet at the hospital coffee shop every day after work, so she can practice English for the price of a coffee. Her son is always with her, playing with trucks and action figures. A real little boy, he is.

I wonder what Ricky was like when he was young. Did he like to play with trucks? Did he give his mother a hard time? Ricky is still a mystery to me—he doesn't seem quite human.

One day Eloise is not at the coffee shop when I go there after work. I wait twenty minutes and she doesn't show up. Feeling a little let down, I decide I will ask Justine for Eloise's phone number the next day. But when I get to work, Eloise is there, smiling and breathless.

"So sorry," she says straightaway. "I went to doctor yesterday....For my son, no for me."

"That's okay Eloise," I say. "But maybe we should exchange phone numbers?"

"Yes, yes!" she says. "You call me."

That night Eloise calls *me*. Her son is in bed, she says in a hushed tone. She just wants to thank me for my help.

"Eloise," I say. "It's nothing."

Eloise is quiet for a moment. "No, Joan," she says. "Is something. Good night, sleep tight, don't let bug beds bite."

Thirty-nine

Ricky and I are getting along at work, although his presence reminds me of Edna and how much I miss her. At the same time, when I think about how Edna had managed to hide from me in the last years of her life, even in the midst of her dementia, I feel cast aside, set adrift. Why was I not worthy of hearing the things she had told my mother, and perhaps even the things she told Ricky?

I watch Ricky as he spoons apple sauce into bowls. He is slow, methodical. Maybe it is his imperturbable cheerfulness, his very mildness, that attracted Edna. To me, it is suspect but perhaps to her it was reassuring.

I step beside him. He glances over at me, surprised. "What did Edna tell you before she died?" I ask. He looks embarrassed. "I mean, did she tell you about Tibor?"

Ricky turns toward me. "Joan," he says patiently, "You need to let it go."

I explode. "You can't tell me that. You don't know—Edna was my—it just doesn't make sense," I sputter. "Why would she not tell me about you? Why would she hide—I don't understand," I say, my hands flying up in the air.

"She knew you'd be upset," Ricky says, turning back to the apple sauce, "but she needed to do what she did."

How is it possible that Ricky Hauser is telling me this, defending Edna from me? I fish a cough drop out of my pocket.

It is unwrapped, with bits of fuzz sticking to it, but I put it in my mouth.

Ricky seems to realize that now is not the time to convince me of anything. He starts to pour milk into plastic cups.

"Let me do it," I say forcefully. He nods, and takes the applesauce out to the waiting residents.

As the double doors flap back and forth, my trembling hands spill milk here and there on the counter. I don't want Ricky to know I am upset, I don't want him to know anything about me.

That afternoon as I leave to meet Eloise at the hospital coffee shop, it occurs to me that it is odd, that Ricky has ended up working at Mount Pleasant around the same time as me. Is it some sort of strange coincidence, or has he engineered things that way? I can't figure out why he would take the job, or how it even came to be offered to him. Maybe Justine had seen him visiting Edna and knew he was good with seniors.

When Eloise arrives, she is alone. "*Henri est avec son ami,*" she says. Her face looks tired and drawn, and she rubs her cast as though it hurts.

"What's wrong, Eloise?" I ask.

She waves her hand in front of her face, as if to say, it's nothing. But I know Eloise enough to realize something is wrong.

"Are you having problems with Henri?" I ask. Eloise looks up, as though begging the heavens not to let her cry. She takes my hands in hers.

"I come to this country," she says. "I have nothing. My husband...dead. My *maman*, my *papa*, all dead. I take Henri and run away." Eloise looks down.

I feel a thrumming in my chest. "Do you mean they all died in Canada?" I ask.

Eloise shakes her head. "No, no, in Congo. All dead by rebels," she says flatly, as though to get it out of the way.

Henri was only a pre-schooler when men came to her door

in the night and left with her husband. She stayed awake all night, hoping he would come back. But in the morning when she went outside, she saw blood on the stones and knew that he would not come home again.

Eloise rubs her face with her hands, as though she is tired.

"I'm so sorry," I tell her. What more could a person say?

Eloise continues. She knew she would have to leave the house and take Henri somewhere safe. Her husband's brother offered her and Henri a room in his house, but he had two wives and a number of children. Eloise knew that she would be expected to be their servant, or worse. She refused and instead packed a suitcase.

Her husband had hidden some money under a stone near the house. It was an ordinary enough looking stone, but he made sure it looked as if it had never been turned. Eloise took the roll of bills from the plastic bag and tucked them into her bra.

She took her daughter to her sister in the next town. I hold my breath. Eloise has a daughter?

Eloise begins to cry. "She is a baby," Eloise says. "Only four years old. My sister tell me she is sick. She need medicine. And I must send money. So I send." Eloise puts her head on the table, and pounds her fist. "But she is too sick. She must go to hospital. But the road is too dangerous—too many attacks. I am afraid she die."

Eloise looks down at her hands, palms facing upward. *Henri ne comprends pas.* He want Xbox, pizza, new bicycle. He don't know we are poor. He forget his sister."

My head is full. There isn't room for anything else.

"I wanted bring my girl to Canada," Eloise says bitterly. "But I was afraid for my boy. He is old enough now that the rebels want take him. My sister, she no have child. I give her my girl." Eloise slaps her forehead. "My baby, my girl," she moans.

I don't know what to do with her grief. It is so much bigger than anything I've ever felt. *Eloise*, I want to say. I hold both her hands.

She smiles at me through her tears, even now. The crinkles at the corners of her eyes are like wings. She pats my hands.

"That is my story Joan. Sad, yes?" She sighs, and gulps. I feel that she is wrung dry of tears. "Now you tell me you story," Eloise says. "Something pretty. Something to make me forget."

What can I tell her? That I have been a misfit since high school? That I am angry at Edna for dying and for keeping her secret from me? I mumble something about not having a story.

"Not true," Eloise says, looking hurt. "Everyone has story."

It grieves me to know I've hurt her. I start speaking, a rambling tale that covers my childhood and Edna's lessons and my parents' courtship. Eloise listens avidly. Her eyes shine when I tell her about the Chinese wedding that almost took place in the bowling alley, and the story of my birth. I tell her my mother's joke, about how the whole hospital, including the doctor, ambulance and even the administrator came to her. She doesn't laugh, but looks deep in thought.

Finally I tell her about Edna keeping her secret from me. Eloise looks at me kindly, and shakes her head.

"Is very hard," she says, "to leave a child." My face reddens. I have forgotten that she also has such a story. She wags her finger gently at me, just as Edna had always done. "You must remember good, and forget bad," Eloise says.

It seems to me that maybe Edna had said some such thing—or maybe Dr. Bard? Forget the bad. Most of the days I've known her, Eloise has done just that. Today she broke down, but I can see she is gathering herself, to go forward, face radiant. And that's what Edna did too. She waved her hand, her heavy arm swinging back and forth. Be happy, she said. Today is a good day.

Forty

My parents are at it again. Deep in conversation at the kitchen table. I am used to them keeping their distance, barely speaking to one another but lately it seems they find the need to talk. Both of them look at me as I come in the front door, their heads turning away from one another.

I sit down with them. The three of us together at one time—I feel a little trickle of happiness.

"Joan." My father's eyes are soupy and tender. "Your mother and I...have decided to separate." My mother isn't looking at me, but down at the table cloth. She is playing with a fork.

I stand up, and go to the sink for a glass of water, then sit back down. Expecting that my father will tell me it is only a joke. But he is looking down at the tablecloth too.

Keeping his eyes on the brown, flowery pattern, my father says, "We've been discussing it for awhile. We didn't want to tell you until we were sure. Your mother would like to keep this house, and you are welcome to stay with her if you wish." Welcome to stay with her? Isn't this my home too? I feel a mist of fear rising off my stomach.

"But we would help you if you want to move out. Now that you have a full-time job, that should be easier. Your mother and I both think it's time you consider your future, since we're not going to be around forever, and this might be a time to... look at your options."

Edna is staring at me from behind my father's head. She has her arms crossed across her breast, and she is waiting for me to say something.

All I can manage is a squeak. "Why...?"

My father shifts his chair and clears his throat. "Well, we've been...it hasn't been easy, for a long time now," he says. He doesn't say, since before you were born, but I hear it like an echo in my head.

Then my mother blurts out, without looking at either of us, "Our hearts aren't in it anymore." And I see in a flash that these past thirty years or so of my life, they've stayed together, while drifting inexorably apart, for my sake.

I look down at the tablecloth, my eyes blurry. For some reason, I think of Eloise dancing with her mop. The people who loved her are dead and she has flown her home with a child in tow, to some strange country of snow and ice, where she must learn a new tongue to survive. But her dance is not tragic or agonized—it is a light-hearted waltz that sweeps her across the floor on invisible wings. She is laughing, bubbling even. Today, this moment, she has forgotten her worries. Today she is happy.

Dr. Bard doesn't think there's anything wrong with me. "Joan," he says, touching my hand and looking deep into my eyes with his tender blue ones. "You've experienced major losses recently. Your last job. Edna dying, and now your parents splitting up." He shakes his head. "You've been doing amazingly well. AND," he says with dramatic emphasis, "You've been moderate on the cough drop usage." He sits back in his chair. "I rest my case," he says, twinkly-eyed.

Dr. Bard doesn't know anything about my anger. He doesn't know that I have just heard Eloise's terrible tale, and that it is keeping me awake at night. He doesn't know that I am shaken to my bones and all I have are the cough drops. It occurs to me that maybe Dr. Bard has spent too long in the Indian sun and his brain has shrivelled like a raisin.

I wonder where my vitriol has come from. It feels poisonous, like an oil spill. Could it be that I have been hanging on to my anger as though it were a precious object instead of a bitter fruit?

My parents are walking away from something that had made them happy once. But I have to remember, they haven't walked away from me. Was it better that they did it now, after having raised me, or like Edna and Eloise, who disappeared before their children could remember?

It doesn't matter, I decide. It is all leaving. And each of them had left someone they loved, not out of malice or neglect, but for reasons that are very good. It is painful to realize that sometimes the best possible outcome is the one where someone was left alone. Even the way Edna left me, I realize, was the best she thought she could do.

Though her mind was getting lost in the clouded whorls of her brain, she remembered she didn't want to endanger our relationship. So she left the story of Tibor for my mother to tell, and hoped I would forgive her, now that her body lies in the cold ground.

I realize that Edna had been afraid to tell me about Tibor. That's the astounding thing. I had thought Edna was unstoppable, a force of nature, wholly unafraid. But in fact, she was an old woman, weak and ill and living her last days without the full use of her mind. She must have realized, even so, that the end was coming, and that the thing between us left unsaid was like a ship without a captain, destined to run aground.

I can't blame her. My mother had said I was conservative and I suppose it is true. No wonder Edna thought I would disown her if I knew about Tibor.

And as for my parents, they had dutifully brought me up. They had spent thirty years of their lives, each one holding my hand. If they are leaving now it is because they can't stay any longer, that they have spent the last bit of the energy of the love between them.

My parents would always be there, I think, just in separate rooms in the house of my life. And Edna—I will carry her photo with me, so that everywhere I go, she will also be there. Forget the bad, remember the good, Eloise had said.

Edna stands on the stern of a ship. Just as she gazed backward at the land of her birth when she left her son and husband fifty years ago, she is watching me as the vessel pulls from shore. She waves a handkerchief at me as I stand and let her leave, raising a hand in farewell, until she is nothing but a dot on the horizon.

Forty-one

I finally come down with the flu that both Eloise and Ricky had. For several days, I lie in bed, and my mother brings me chicken soup, which I can barely eat. Then one day I wake up feeling stronger, and ravenous. I have bacon and eggs for breakfast, with my mother looking on happily.

I call Justine to tell her I will be back to work but by the time I reach Mount Pleasant I am half an hour late. I apologize to Justine, who fixes me with a grim look, her spiky hair sticking out all over like a sea urchin. Ricky is already getting snack ready when I come in the door.

"Sorry Ricky," I say, pulling on my hairnet.

Ricky turns to me and smiles. "No problemo," he says cheerily. I nearly laugh in his face. "It's good you're better," he says, turning away from me, humming a song that I recognize.

"What is that?" I say.

Ricky thinks for a moment. "Hickory Dickory Dock?" he says, looking sheepish. Eloise has turned us both into babies. I punch Ricky Hauser in the arm.

"It's not pre-school, Hauser," I say. He looks surprised, then reddens, and smiles.

I catch myself humming also, a tuneless song, that seems to rise from inside my chest. It is the kind of song I would sing at the beach, a song from inside the wind and surf which no one but myself can hear. It is the song that tells me I am happy.

"Eloise was here this morning and asked me to tell you something," Ricky says.

"Is it something good, or something bad?"

"Well, it's…a bit of both."

I feel my shoulders slump. "Why doesn't she tell me herself?"

Ricky pours milk into cups. "She—well she's going back to the Congo."

I stop in my tracks.

"She's taking a doctor with her, to look after her daughter. Well, not just her daughter. She's got help from a local organization to bring medical supplies to her village. She says it is because of the story you told. About when you were born and the hospital came to your house."

I stand with my mouth open. "That was just days ago…how did she…?"

"I guess her own GP volunteered to go," Ricky says. "He was looking for a volunteer position overseas for a couple months when Eloise talked to him about her daughter, and it just went from there."

It seems impossible. But somehow, it also makes sense. Eloise has a magic touch—she turns hearts to gold.

I stand motionless for a few minutes, thinking. Ricky points at the cups. "We need a few more of these," he says.

We serve snack and sit at our usual tables. Mrs. Oliver's head shakes "no" when I ask her if she wants the bread spread with Cheez Whiz. But she says, in a tremulous voice, "Yes, dear. I'm starving." Mrs. Johnson, as usual, sits with her hands in her lap, and her mouth open like a baby bird.

Mrs. Oliver seems to want to talk. "My grandson is coming today," she says. "It's my birthday."

I sit back, surprised. "Is that right?" I ask. "No one told me."

Mrs. Oliver pats my hand. "Don't worry dear," she says, her voice fading. "When you get this old, birthdays seem a bit redundant." She smiles a jiggly smile.

I laugh and think about how long I've sat with Mrs. Oliver without knowing about her sense of humour. It is a tragedy, really.

That afternoon Ricky and I make a birthday cake for Mrs. Oliver. It is only a cake mix with pudding in it, but it smells delicious coming out of the oven. Ricky finds some birthday candles in a drawer, and we cover the cake with them. Justine sticks her head in the door and frowns.

"Mrs. Oliver's birthday," I explain. She puts a hand over her mouth. Residents are supposed to be given a decorated store-bought cake, but clearly, no one had remembered.

When Mrs. Oliver sees her cake, she smiles. "Looks home-made," she says. Justine turns red.

"Actually, it's from a mix," I say.

"As long as there's ice cream," Mrs. Oliver rattles. There isn't, but Justine rushes to her office where she has a small fridge with a few ice cream bars in the freezer. We manage to pry one off its stick and plop it down in the middle of a wedge of cake.

Mrs. Oliver smiles. "Ahh," she says, "That looks good." And it is. I feed her and Mrs. Johnson while at the same time working on my own piece of cake. I figure that now I know what it feels like to be a mother of twins, and that I'm really not interested.

Eloise shows up for her last pay cheque half-way through the afternoon, while Ricky is preparing snack and I am clean-ing the washroom. When I return to the kitchen, she is cra-dling her broken arm and speaking in soft, urgent tones to Ricky, who shakes his head. When she sees me, she bursts into a smile that sends a wash of gladness through me.

"Joan!" she cries. "Joan." She wraps her good arm around my shoulders and kisses me hard on the cheek. Her excite-ment is like electricity, running through her to the ends of her hair, through my shoulder into my chest.

"I go home," she says, her eyes wet.

"I know," I say. "I am glad for you."

Eloise wipes her nose. "I miss you."

"I'll miss you too, Eloise," I say, and think for a moment. "Will you be safe?"

Eloise nods. "I think so." She crosses her fingers. "I will be with the doctor. Henri will stay here, with family of his friend." Her eyes look pained, and I know it is because she is tugged between her two children, each pulling her in the opposite direction.

Justine comes through the kitchen door with Eloise's cheque. "Here you are," she says primly. Eloise gives her a hug, and Justine's mouth softens. "Let's let these two get back to work, eh?"

As she ushers Eloise out the door, Eloise looks over her shoulder at me and raises her hand with two fingers crossed.

"No bug beds," she says. I raise my hand, fingers crossed, in a farewell salute.

By the end of the day, Ricky and I are both tired. We each mop a bathroom and then the kitchen floor and that finishes us. Ricky sits on a step stool, takes his hairnet off, and shakes out his dirty blonde locks. He looks like a teenage headbanger, I think, as I pull on my coat.

"Hey," he says, blushing. "Do you want to grab a bite to eat?" I stop in my tracks—is he asking me out on a date?

"My treat," he says, miserably. I feel powerful, and know I can't abuse my power.

"Sure," I say. "That would be nice." He smiles gratefully.

Ricky's truck is a '92 Ford that has seen enough. He cleans off the front seat for me and piles the junk that had been on it into the back. I wonder how he can afford to drive a truck, on the salary we are getting. As though he reads my mind he says, "I'll be doing my own work come spring. I guess Justine will be looking for two more people, with both Eloise and me gone."

I feel like I've been punched in the stomach. It hasn't hit me till then that of course Eloise would be gone…and now Ricky too. Am I the only one who doesn't know how to move on?

Ricky drives us to Fast Food Lane as we called it in high school. We have the choice of all the major fast food outlets.

"I'd like the biggest burger it's possible to get," I say. "Where would that be?" We both think for a moment. "I might have to kill a cow," I say.

We end up at a pizza place, where there are red and white checked plastic tablecloths. There is donair meat turning on a spit and a juke box.

"I'm really glad you came out with me, Joan," Ricky says.

I squirm a little in my seat. "It's been a long time since high school," I say.

Ricky nods, thankfully nonplussed by my non sequitur. "It's been really great working with you," he says, looking down. "I'm used to working on my own, in my business."

I think of all the jobs I've been in, and how I don't know whether it's better to work with someone or alone. There is just a lot I don't know, I think.

We order a pizza and find out we like the same toppings— bacon, pineapple and hot peppers.

"What are the odds of that?" Ricky wonders aloud, eyes wide. I want to laugh again but he is clearly serious. What *are* the odds of that, I wonder to myself.

Ricky puts a quarter in the jukebox, and chooses U2's "Beautiful Day." We listen while we eat, and I feel strangely sad. It might be PMS or the guy in the kitchen chopping onions, but I think it's just that it really is a beautiful day, and that something is coming to an end. My parents splitting up, Edna dying, Eloise leaving, and the fact that soon Ricky will be gone.

After a little while it seems that maybe we've said all that can be said. We sit back in our booth and gaze out the window at the headlights of cars in the drizzle. Ricky clears his throat.

"There's something I've been wanting to tell you," he says. I wait. "Edna was in pain, after her surgery to amputate her leg." I know that and it pierces me. Why is he telling me now? "Her stump pained her. So I helped her," he says, looking down. I stare at him, uncomprehending. "She took marijuana in the morning and evening," he says, "supplied by me. I just wanted to tell you that, in the interest of full disclosure."

I sit back and look at him. Out of the jumble of thoughts comes a clear voice. Edna's. *He helped me*, she says. *Forgive him*.

Ricky's face is pale with two red spots on his cheeks. I take his hand, awkwardly. "Thank you for helping her," I say shakily.

Ricky's face brightens. He reaches into his pocket and pulls out an envelope, fingers it for a few moments, then passes it to me. My first thought is that I am afraid to open it, in case it is a love letter.

"It's from Edna," he says. I feel a brief a twinge of disappointment, but then my mind begins to turn over. From Edna? I look at him. "I don't know what it's about," Ricky says. "Edna asked me to give you this letter after she died." He looks sheepish. "It took me awhile to find the right moment."

I gaze at him for a long time. Should I be upset or angry, I wonder. But I'm not. I feel as though I've been hit over the head with a baseball bat. Ricky is still unfathomable to me, but at the moment, it hardly matters.

I tuck the letter away in the pocket of my jacket. Ricky watches it disappear inside my coat, and looks longingly after it. I don't want to share my moment with Edna with anyone.

Ricky drives me home and my mother and father are standing at the living room window watching as he walks me to the door. Ricky holds out his hand to me. I take it and hold it. I hear my father clearing his throat as he comes to open the door to let me in.

"Thank you, Ricky," I say. "I had a very nice time." It is true, even if, in the end, he had told me the last thing I wanted to know about Edna.

Ricky smiles and turns away, as my father peers out the screen door at him.

"Who was that?" my father asks, eyes brows contracting. I smile and shake my head.

"It was...no one," I say. "A friend."

That night, as I lie in bed I open Edna's letter. I try to prolong the moment, reading my name again and again on the outside of the envelope, savouring Edna's delicate script. But eventually curiosity wins out. When I open it, several crisp hundred dollar bills flutter out.

I count the bills. There are ten of them. I feel cold and shaky, and wrap the blanket around me.

Edna's letter is on onion skin paper, which I have not seen for many years.

Dear Joan,

How are you? I am fine. I ask Ricky to give you this letter when I am gone.

He is a good boy, I know he will do it.

I am dead when you read this. I think you will meet my son, Tibor. I tell him about you and that you are like a daughter to me. He never had a sister, and you never had a brother. Now you do. I hope and pray.

I ask your mother to tell you my story when I die. She promise me.

I think you know about Josef's father.

Here there is a splotch as though Edna had wept—or maybe spat. The letter continues in another ink.

I ask you a favour. I want you to go to Hungary, to give Josef a letter from me. It tells why I left him. I don't want Tibor to know this. You work for Tibor, help him with English. He wants to do import, export. But it is for Josef to tell the rest. His father is dead many years now. Maybe he will be not so angry and ashamed. In the letter, I tell him I loved him, he was my first love, and I always sorry I hurt him so much.

I hope you still knitting. I want give you some advice. Be kind. Finish something that you start. Don't be afraid.

Something inside me crumbles, like a tower of sand.

You are a good girl. I watch you from Heaven, I hope.

Your Edna

The last page of the letter is in Hungarian, for Josef. I read the letter three times, then I put it back in the envelope, along with the money, and put it under my pillow. I am shivering, my nose running, my heart racing. Somehow Edna has reached across the chasm of time to put things right. Though it hurts to know that this is her last missive to me, I feel buoyed up, as though I am floating on the surface of the sea.

Now it is up to me. Edna has asked me to go to Hungary, with her letter to Josef, and I can't refuse. No matter how frightened I feel, how unlikely a world traveler I am, my job is to fly across the ocean with this precious letter. *Don't be afraid*, Edna had written, as if she could feel my fear. Her eyes are on me. She knows that the only thing I had left of her was love, and that it is enough.

Forty-two

Ricky is already in the kitchen when I enter. He turns to look at me, his face bathed in light.

"I'm giving my two weeks' notice, Ricky," I say. "I'm going to Hungary."

He stands there with his mouth open, like a baby bird. "When will you go?" he asks quietly, his face pale.

"Two weeks," I say. It hasn't occurred to me that Ricky would be upset. We had barely held hands. "I'll email," I say lamely. "I'll send you a postcard." Ricky smiles, barely. My face hot, I punch him in the arm. "Hauser, don't make me cry. You're the first person I've told."

We work in silence for a few minutes, then Ricky turns to me.

"I always liked you, you know," he says, smiling, embarrassed. "Even in high school when you thought I was a pot-head."

My heart is like a race car, zooming ahead. What if I stopped here? If I simply decide to forget the things Edna has asked of me, and nestle here with Ricky in this industrial kitchen? Edna had said to follow my heart. She had almost thrown us together. It seems as though she had hoped for such an ending.

But what she has asked of me, a simple favour that I could choose to ignore, is the other path, the one that leads from her heart to mine. It is the path through the mountains of Edna's past, one that will point me, like an arrow, to Josef.

Edna is asking me for one more act of kindness. It is a job for which she has paid me all my life, with her fierce love. I will not fail her, even though the tree of my courage is shaking in the breeze.

I feel like an ice cream cone, melting in the sun, a solid becoming liquid. So many things might have been different.

I give Justine my notice in writing before I leave that afternoon. Her mouth is set firmly against me, and her spiky hair seems to stiffen.

"It's for Edna," I blurt. "I have to go." I must look miserable. Justine's mouth is still hard but her eyes soften. She smiles slightly. "I'm sorry Justine," I say. "I know I've let you down."

She just shakes her head slightly. "We've all got things we need to do in this life," she says. It surprises me that she understands.

"Here," she says, reaching into her desk. "Maybe you can give these to Tibor, since you're going." She pulls out some photographs of Edna's wake. There is Tibor, standing beside me as I give my farewell speech to Edna. He is listening intently and his eyes look kind. Another photo shows Tibor, Justine and me, and the corner of Edna's casket. I can see her wispy curls. She is resting, waiting for her soul to be set free, to fly into the boundless air.

"This one's for you," Justine says, handing me one more photo. It is of Ricky and me, talking for the first time at the wake. His hand is open, gesturing toward me and I am looking down, at my feet. Look up, I tell myself. Look up at the man who will deliver your future. But it is already too late.

Over supper at McDonald's, I tell my parents about my plan. My mother's fish sandwich is halfway to her mouth, and my father stops chewing his bite of Big Mac. My mouth full of hamburger I explain, "I'm going to help Tibor with his business." I had called him the day before, the distance crackling between us. I imagined the satellite, its mirrors deflecting my phone signal from outer space down to a telephone in Budapest.

"Joan!" Tibor shouted, and laughed. "Is good to hear you."

"I want to come to Hungary," I said. "For work."

"Yes, come, come to my country. I find you English teaching, and you help me with business." I imagined him trying to wink. "You bring boyfriend?"

"No," I said. "My boyfriend...I don't have a boyfriend now."

"Oh I am sorry," he said, with real concern. He is quiet for a moment. "Your mother? She have boyfriend?"

I thought of my mother, her bangles jingling on her arm. My father is moving out the week I am to leave Canada.

"Yes, she is seeing someone," I said. It could be true.

"Oh," said Tibor, sounding deflated. But then he laughed. "She is happy I think. "

"Yes, she is happy," I told him. And it is true. My mother's eyes have been shinier and her step lighter of late. It is strange that my parents deciding to separate has given them both a new lease on life.

"I am happy too. I happy you come to Budapest. If you work as teacher they give you room, maybe even flat. But you stay with me first. I have very nice chesterfield."

Tibor is Edna's son. I will tell him about all the things she had done for me, the cakes she had baked, the chores she gave me at the Jamiesons' house, the bottle of gin under the sink and the little crucifix she wore that touched my cheek when she hugged me to her bosom. It occurs to me that maybe Edna loved me so much because she couldn't hold her own son, the dark-eyed boy she left behind when she came to Canada. Tibor was that boy, now almost an old man. For Edna's sake, I will help him to know her as I had. I will be the satellite, transmitting her love for him with the mirrors of my stories.

Perhaps this has been her plan all along. But that thought dissolves, like foam on the sea's edge. It is just life, the way life unfolds. Edna hadn't known, and neither had I. Just as Ricky didn't know the content of Edna's letter would send me far away from him. Life is such a mountainous country, with narrow footpaths and countless peaks and bends, that we can often see only what was directly in front of us.

My parents look at one another, across the gulf of time. I am the baby, floating down the river in a basket. They call to one another to grab hold of me, but each of them were too far from the river. Helpless, they watch me go. My parents, receding from me like the shore from the sea.

"As long as you're happy," says my mother, and her voice seems to come from far away.

"Do you need our help?" comes my father's voice, faint on the wind.

"No," I call to them, "I think I'll be fine."

I call Dr. Bard to tell him that I am leaving. There is silence on his end of the phone.

"Thanks," I say, " for the advice."

Dr. Bard clears his throat and for once, I think, he is at a loss for words. Finally he says, "You're doing a brave thing, Joan." It seems like he is already a thousand miles away. "Safe journey," he tells me, waving from the shore of my past.

Forty-three

S oon after I arrive in Hungary, Ricky sends me a postcard, saying that he misses me at Mount Pleasant and that Mrs. Oliver died in her sleep the day I left. There is never any other destination than the ash pit, no matter what mountains we climb, but it is not a sad thing, as I once thought. Shedding our bodies and leaving them on the shore comes before slipping naked into a pool at midnight, with nothing to impede our swimming but our own fear of darkness.

Tibor had welcomed me at the airport, and driven me, the Danube River winking between the endless, centuries-old buildings, to his flat in a four-storey house. He is the same Tibor, like Edna but without her fire. His mildness and his eyes' lack of focus disturb me, and I wonder if it might be a product of alcoholism. He tells me he has set up an interview for me at a language school the next day. But tonight, after I've had rest, he wants to take me for dinner at his father's farm. His father, Josef, is an old man but his wits are sharp.

Tibor's flat is simply furnished and very neat. A Bible lies on the coffee table. I fall asleep and wake up a couple hours later. Tibor is sitting at the kitchen table, reading the Bible and drinking a glass of red wine.

On the drive to Josef's farm, I imagine Josef and Edna as a young couple, driving happily together toward their doom. The farmhouse is just as dusty and neglected looking on the outside as my mother had described. I feel afraid to go inside. There is Josef, an old man, sitting in front of the fire while his younger sister, an old woman who has never married, stirs a pot on the stove. When Tibor and I come through the door, they look at me, unblinking. Tibor kisses them both extravagantly. Josef, sour, turns his face away, while Ekaterina indulges Tibor with a soft, powdered cheek.

Tibor shows me the back garden. I imagine Josef's young sisters peering at Edna from the doorway. He shows me the bedrooms. Where Aunt Ekaterina sleeps now, and where I imagine Edna had been raped by Josef's father, there is a single neat bed, covered in an old quilt, a rosary hanging over the iron headboard. It is a low-ceilinged room with wooden beams and no sign of Edna—her presence is nowhere in this house.

Tibor and I sit at the table across from Josef and eat the rye bread and goulash the old aunt puts in front of us. Tibor tries to make conversation with Josef but the old man just spoons his food into his mouth steadily, as though he is moving a pile of rocks. Eventually Tibor stops trying and eats in silence, bright eyed.

At the end of the meal, Josef grunts something at me. Tibor stops eating and answers in a stream of Hungarian.

"My father asks, why have you come?" he says, without a trace of embarrassment. "I tell him you want to work as English teacher and you come to help my business. Is true, no? My father doesn't understand, why young people want come to this country."

Tibor stands up. "Thank you Auntie, that was delicious," he says and nods to her, repeating his words in Hungarian. I nod agreement, and she smiles. He turns to me. "Excuse me, Joan, I must go to toilet." And he steps out into the back garden. I can see an outhouse there at the end of the yard.

I turn to Josef, who is drinking a glass of beer and staring grimly at me. I pull out Edna's letter.

"For you," I say, "from Edna." He looks back at me, uncomprehending. "From Orsolia," I say. He takes it and reads it. I watch his eyes widen, scanning back and forth over Edna's words, his hard mouth beginning to droop at the corners. As Tibor walks back toward the house, he tucks it into the pocket of his shirt.

When we leave for the city, Tibor's aunt pats my cheeks. And Josef stands, slightly stooped, and kisses my hand. Then he shakes it. It seems he doesn't want to let go, as if he needs to say something to me or needs to hear me say something. I shake his hand once, hard, and look into his eyes. *Orsolia*.

There were mourning doves on the roof, crooning softly as darkness fell. *Be kind*, she says. *Finish what you start. And don't be afraid*.

I call my mother the day I start working at a language school in Budapest to let her know the good news. She is in a hurry, she says, because she is going on a date.

"With who?" I ask her. I can hear her eyelashes flickering.

"With Dr. Bard," she says. "Now don't get upset...." I hold the receiver in my hand and look at it. What am I hearing?

"Joan," my mother calls, "Are you there? Dr. Bard—Allen—asked me out one day after your father and I...after he'd spoken with you about you going away," she says. I feel my stomach loosen. "He said it was an unusual situation, but since he knew you would be leaving his practice to go to Hungary, he thought it was alright." I hear her catch her breath. *He* thought it was alright. No one had bothered to ask *me*.

Edna stares at me from a picture frame on Tibor's coffee table. I see Eloise with her mop, soundlessly sweeping across the kitchen doorway. They are waiting for me to say something.

I take a breath. "Okay, Ma. I hope you have a good time with Dr. Bard. Allen," I say.

There is silence. My mother must have dropped the phone. "What did you say, sweetie," she asks finally, her voice trembling.

I try again. "Ma, I hope you have a good time with...Allen." I can tell my mother is emotional.

"Thanks darling," she says gratefully. "I'll tell Allen you're doing fine and say hello."

I didn't, I think—but all I say is "Bye, Ma."

It is part of growing up, I think, and it is hard. To be able to give your mother permission to date your therapist. To watch your parents change partners and waltz across the dance floor in someone else's arms, and cheer them on. Edna and Eloise stand with me and clap as my parents take their bows and go to stand in a line with my ancestors, watching me. They aren't heavy—they are as light as a feather. I put them in my briefcase, and set off for work, the Danube winking in the sun.

There is a pair of swans on the river, necks intertwined. I stop to feed them some bread from my lunch. They nibble delicately, then turn their backs on me, gliding away from the riverbank. Respectful of their privacy, I turn and keep walking. After a minute, there is a soft sound in the air, and looking up, I see the swans flying above the river. Their wings are a velvet accordion, turning the air into a tuneless music. I stop, my hand shading my eyes, my heart glad. I will remember this day, long after my last memory is stamped in my brain, long after my life has been worn to a sliver. I step out of the waters of my past and shake my feathers, drops of water falling everywhere like tears.

Acknowledgements

There are many people who deserve my thanks but none more so than these: Thanks to Sue Goyette's marathon fiction class, 2006-2007, whose critiques and enthusiasm kept me going; to Emma Foulger, Leslie Hennen and Selena Nemorin for your encouraging noises and friendship; to The Nova Scotia Mental Health Foundation and the Department of Tourism, Culture and Heritage for their generous grants, which enabled me to attend Summer Literary Seminars (SLS) in St. Petersburg, Russia in 2006; to SLS Russia participants and faculty, whose feedback inspired me to finish; to my family, whose unfailing support, financial and otherwise, also helped make that trip possible, along with that other, bigger trip—the one that takes us from day to day, day after day; to Wayne Johnston whose book "The Story of Bobby O'Malley" made me laugh my guts out and sat in my brain while I began this novel; to my shrink, Dr. Nancy Robertson, for helping to keep my mind mostly upright; to my Healthy Minds Cooperative writing group who inspire me to keep writing and laughing; to my friends and the wonderful women of the mental health community in Halifax, especially Kristine Erglis, Sheila Morrison and Susan Roper; to Chow Ping Yip, who allowed me to work on this novel while employed as a retail clerk in her store, Silver Silk; a huge thanks to Robbie MacGregor and Nicholas Boshart of Invisible Publishing for their tireless support; and another to Stephanie Domet, indomitable editor—I couldn't have done it without you!

Invisible Publishing is committed to working with writers who might not ordinarily be published and distributed commercially. We work exclusively with emerging and under-published authors to produce entertaining, affordable, books.

We believe that books are meant to be enjoyed by everyone and that sharing our stories is important. In an effort to ensure that books never become a luxury, we do all that we can to make our books more accessible.

We are collectively organized and our production processes are transparent. At Invisible, publishers and authors recognize a commitment to one another, and to the development of communities which can sustain and encourage storytellers.

If you'd like to know more please get in touch.
info@invisiblepublishing.com

Invisible Publishing
Halifax & Toronto